About the Author

Born in North Carolina, the author spent all but one year of life living in Arizona. He is a graduate from Arizona State with a Bachelor in English Creative Writing and is currently living with his wife, daughter, and several animals. He has had an inspiration for writing since he was eight and have been working toward a working novel since high school.

The Diary of Sarah Jane

Gunnar Anderson

The Diary of Sarah Jane

Olympia Publishers
London

www.olympiapublishers.com
OLYMPIA PAPERBACK EDITION

Copyright © Gunnar Anderson 2024

The right of Gunnar Anderson to be identified as author of
this work has been asserted in accordance with sections 77 and 78 of
the Copyright, Designs and Patents Act 1988.

All Rights Reserved

No reproduction, copy or transmission of this publication
may be made without written permission.
No paragraph of this publication may be reproduced,
copied or transmitted save with the written permission of the publisher,
or in accordance with the provisions
of the Copyright Act 1956 (as amended).

Any person who commits any unauthorized act in relation to
this publication may be liable to criminal
prosecution and civil claims for damage.

A CIP catalogue record for this title is
available from the British Library.

ISBN: 978-1-80439-728-2

This is a work of fiction.
Names, characters, places and incidents originate from the writer's
imagination. Any resemblance to actual persons, living or dead, is
purely coincidental.

First Published in 2024

Olympia Publishers
Tallis House
2 Tallis Street
London
EC4Y 0AB

Printed in Great Britain

Acknowledgements

Thank you to my beautiful wife, Taya for helping me push
through to finishing this novel.

This book deals with graphic accounts of harassment and abuse. These instances may be intense for some readers.

Big Bad World

I woke up, and hopped down the stairs to the living room with a J.K. Rowling book pressed tightly to my torso in my arms. It was a gift from my dad for my eighth birthday as were the soft unicorn pajamas that I had gotten from my mother. If I were able to, I would have been reading as I climbed down. Her writing was amazing and I was beginning to really enjoy the magical world that she created and the main characters made me feel like an equal, like I wasn't the only one who got picked on, on a daily basis. My parents were already downstairs; my father with his coffee and his toast and my mother elbows deep in the morning's dirty breakfast dishes. They weren't married, but they still managed to get along for my sake.

"Good morning, sweetie. Did you sleep well?" I shrugged my shoulders and set my book down on the table then climbed into my usual seat. I flipped the book open to page one sixty-four to continue reading where I left off. It hurt to force my eyes to focus on the page. I would get really bad headaches, but my love for reading was greater than the pain.

"Where are your glasses, sweetheart?" my mother asked, leaving the dirty dishes, I knew, she would just dump into the dishwasher later. I stared at her for a moment before I answered her.

"I didn't want to wear them," I finally admit.

"How come?" she pressed. I shrugged my shoulders. She came over and closed the book in front of me. "Well, go and get your glasses. You look like you're in pain trying to read without them." I sighed and began pushing around my breakfast instead.

"Your mother's right, pumpkin," my dad added, pointing his coffee at me before taking a sip. "Go ahead and eat your breakfast, then get ready for school. I'll drop you off on my way to the office." I nodded without another word as I ate my toast and eggs. They were as bland as ever, just as my trip to school was when my dad drove.

It was always quiet in my dad's truck when he drove me. I would hear him and my mother talk about getting a new car, but he constantly brought up the fact that his truck had sentimental value. Trees flew past my window, and I tried my best to follow them with my eyes to make out their shapes and what kind they were. This went on for five minutes before my dad cleared his throat.

"So, are you ready for your first day back, sweetheart?" My eyes skipped a tree and fell on the white picket fence.

"I guess," I said with a shrug.

"What do you mean? You've always liked school."

"Doesn't mean I like the people," I mumbled. He glanced at me with a raised eyebrow. "What?" He sighed and gave his focus back to the road.

"You're weird," he chimed with a light chuckle.

"I am your child," I shot back. A small smirk formed on my lips before going back to the trees.

"There's my girl," I heard him whisper.

I saw the school appear from around the corner, and I instantly felt my heart in my throat. It was a sight of nightmares. I could not explain them, other than my bullies normally followed me home from the cinderblock prison instead of the typical monsters that kept the other kids up at night. For me, it was the kids in my class that were the monsters. My dad pulled into the drop-off line ready to send me off, but all I heard was a ringing. It took him a couple of calls before I finally heard him.

"Hey!" I finally looked at him. "Are you okay?" I nodded though my heart was beating heavy in my chest. "Okay, sweet pea. Have a great day. Mom, and I will be here to pick you up after school."

"Okay," I said a bit shaky, stepping out of the car.

"I love you!" he called to me, but I was too nervous to reply back or even hear him.

There I was in the elementary school yard; one of the most dangerous places I had ever been. Each year, at least two kids broke their arms jumping off the swings, eleven kids suffered burns from the plastic slides, and not to mention the number of times there was a lice outbreak that I was always lucky to avoid. Not playing or talking to any of the others helped a lot. I walked over to stand in line and wait for our teacher to come take us inside. Many of the others were already out on the playground, with their bags left in line to mark their spots. I was never a fan of the playground. A lot of the structures scared me with how tall they were. Spending my time reading was better anyway. I sat down and pulled out my book to begin where I left off at breakfast, but as soon as I pulled out the bookmark, the bell rang and whistles began to blow on the playground.

Teachers stood in their lines waiting for their students to return. I sighed and put my book back as the others began to crowd around me. I hated being so close to the other students. Having them crowded around me made me nervous, and not knowing any of them did not help either. I had no idea why, but I just did not like being in large crowds, even if it was a room with my family members. The list of things that scared me: large crowds, meeting new people, speaking in front of others, and abruptly loud noises. The waiting lines, as well as the rest of the school, was the visualization of all of it. All the more reason I stayed to myself.

My new teacher, Miss Henderson led us through the halls of the school and up two sets of stairs before finally bringing us into our new classroom for the year. I remembered 'Meet the Teacher Night' and went straight for my seat that was thankfully placed near the window. It was a pretty view. The school was built on the edge of the park, so my view was filled with tall trees, winding dirt paths lined with beautiful flowers, and a pond that was filled with fish. I wished I could draw it, but I was denied by Miss Henderson as she began to take us through our first day of lessons. History, reading comprehension, and writing flew by after I finished my assignments early and went back to reading my book. Being a bookworm definitely had its advantages especially when it came to the quick quizzes that were handed out. I had a knack for it, as my teachers said. Mathematics was the subject I did not enjoy. The entire time was used to explain how and why things worked. It was also time I spent it in a separate classroom in the school's 'Advanced Mathematical Comprehension' class. I was quick to grasp the concepts, but the teacher did not let me read during her lectures. It made no difference. I learned it all from the books anyway. We went out to the playground for lunch and recess, but I spent most of it reading.

The whole day dragged out until the final bell rang and we were marched back out to the playground to wait for our parents. Well, most of us were. The rest went to the buses that drove them home. I sat at the benches waiting for my parents to come and get me, my book opened up in my lap. However, a fight that broke out among the other students grabbed my attention. I did not know why, but someone was unhappy with the other. It escalated quickly, and they began drifting in my direction. Eventually, they were right on top of me, four boys nearly twice my size beating on each other with me wrapped up in the middle of them. I acted on fear and instinct trying to protect myself. In the heat of it, I started swinging my arms trying to get out of the huddle. My hands struck two of them and they went down moaning and out of breath while the other two eventually knocked themselves out. That is when one of the teachers finally came over and saw me standing by them. To make matters worse, I was the only one left standing. I had read enough to know what happened next. Picking up my book that got mindlessly thrown to the ground, I followed the teacher to the office, preparing myself for the conversation between myself, the principal, and my parents, knowing they had to find a new school for me to go to.

*

Fourth grade, private school. The days were longer and the lessons were harder, but I still managed to get passing marks. The place where I was put after two more suspensions in third grade. Fights had become frequent there, and I was always found as a part of them simply from being in the wrong place at the right time. What was I supposed to do? Not fight back and defend myself? At least the people here were nicer. Well, the teachers were at least. The students were jerks and snobs. I wanted to say entitled, but the word was still too new for me. Most of them said they got in on a scholarship, but I did not believe them. They were from the north side of town which meant they had a decent amount of money. My parents were unfortunate enough to *have* to pay for me to be here, simply because of my record. Although they were reluctant to let me in, they liked the way my test scores looked compared to some of their other students.

The uniform was terrible though. I was required to wear khakis and an awful powder blue polo. Backpacks had to be a solid color that was either blue, black, grey, or white. I opted for the black. They occasionally had casual Fridays though where I got to wear a T-shirt... with the same school logo as the polo, and in the same ugly color. At least I could wear whatever shoes I wanted, but they had to be like the backpacks; all one color and no designs; black shoes with white soles it was. My mother scorned me for having to spend so much money. My father was willing to go the extra mile to get me the education I needed, even if it meant getting a second job and picking up extra hours at his first. Private schools were expensive.

One thing that struggled to become normal for me was mandatory physical education, and rainy days brought about no exception. I guess the school had a reputation for its sports program. Being a school with an elementary, middle, and high school, I was not surprised. However, I had no desire to partake in any of the physical activities, and my marks were never the best. They had obstacle courses that got harder as the year went on and as you progressed through the grade levels. Being as small as I was, the courses did not take lightly to me. I was easily the smallest person in my class which was another point of teasing for the other students.

The ropes were the hardest for me. Anything that involved climbing was a weak point for me, which came out to more than half the course. The spring season showers left the ropes wet and slippery. Everyone still managed to climb up and ring the bell with ease. I stared up at the bronze bell while they went one by

16

one without slipping once. It finally came down to my turn.

I gripped the rope and watched as my fingers barely wrapped around it. Throwing my legs around the rope, I began to make my climb toward the bell. My heart was pounding; not just from the previous exercises or the fact that everyone was staring at me. Our times were being recorded for our final scores. I put one hand over the other and did my best to pull myself up with the twigs I had for arms. They began to ache and I could feel my hands slipping and losing both grip and strength.

"Let's go, Cranston! We don't have all day!" Our instructor yelled up at me. I knew my time was not going to be great.

That last name, my mother's last name, and I hated it. I was angry and I began climbing faster. My eyes saw red as I looked toward the bell at the top. It grew closer, and I could feel my adrenaline go through the roof. I reached the top and rang the bell. My lungs were burning and my breath came in heaving gasps. I had finally done it, after nine months of being at this school, but now the fear set in. How am I going to get down? I made a mistake and looked down. Instinctively, my hands gripped the rope even tighter.

"Come on, Miss Cranston! We have others that need to work this course!" The coach was still yelling at me.

I took some deep breaths and began to scale back down, one hand under the other, slowly. One arm extended me downward a little too much, and I felt my hand slip on a spot of wet rope. I tried to grip it tighter with my other hand, but it simply was not enough. Both hands slipped and I fell to the dirt. I hit the ground as a crunching sound echoed in my ears. I did not know if it was my bones or the ground itself. All I remember was blacking out as my ears rang.

When I finally woke up, I was lying in a bright room with a

lot of sounds. Random beeping, people talking quietly, carts rolling around, and a phone that seemed to ring constantly regardless of how many times someone would answer it. Occasionally, I could hear sirens coming from outside while people groaned nearby. It took me a while, but I eventually felt the pain shooting through my arm. Looking around, my eyes finally fell on my dad, tears welling up in my eyes.

"It hurts," I whimpered to him. He came over to me.

"It's okay, sweetie. You'll be okay," he told me. I began to sob slightly and I could not control it. "I'll call the nurse and tell her you're in pain." He hit a small red button on what looked like a remote control.

"What happened?" I asked through ragged breaths.

"You fell off a rope at school and hurt your arm and your shoulder."

"Where's Mom?"

"She's at work, baby."

"Why isn't she here?"

"She told me her boss wouldn't let her leave." This made me want to cry more, and I did.

"It's not fair!" I sobbed. The nurse finally came in.

"Hello, Mister Palmer, is there anything you guys need?"

"Hi. Yes. My daughter is in a lot of pain," he told her. She came over to me and looked me in the eyes.

"Do you want the pain to go away?" she asked me. I nodded. "Okay, sweetie. I'll be right back with some medicine that should help." She rubbed the top of my head before walking out. She had really pretty eyes that reminded me of my mother's. Bright blue eyes with a gold ring that sparkled when she smiled. It helped get rid of some of the pain. She came back only a few seconds later with a shot that she put into a small tube connected to my arm. I could not help, but stare at her.

"There we go. The pain should go away in a little while."

"Okay," I said. "Can you stay with me until then?" I asked.

"Sarah, the nurse has other patients to attend to."

"It's okay, Mister Palmer. It's part of my job after all. And she's such a sweet girl."

"Oh," he said. "Would you like this seat then?"

"It's okay, the examiner's chair is good enough for me."

"Thank you, Miss…"

"Melody."

"Thank you, Miss Melody." It did not take long for the medicine to take over as I began to feel a little drowsy, but I could still hear Dad and Miss Melody talking.

"So, how long have you been doing this?" he asked.

"Is that your way of starting a conversation?"

"It's been a while since I've had to." He let out a chuckle. She did too.

"Oh? And what about Misses Palmer?"

"Never married."

"Ah. That would explain why Sarah doesn't share your last name."

"It does. Now, my question?"

"Well, I finished school a few months ago, so I'm fairly new to being a nurse."

"Huh, you seem too good to be a novice."

"Top of my class, but I don't like to talk about it." There was a short silence.

"So," my dad began again, "between nursing and your home life, is there any free time to, I don't know, go grab some coffee or a bite to eat?"

"Is that a date proposal, Mister Palmer?"

19

"It might be…" They both chucked.

"George?" It was my mother.

"Hey, Jen. You're here."

"Yeah, I'm here." She sounded angry. "Who's this?"

"Oh, I'm Melody, your daughter's nurse."

"Why are you talking to my boyfriend?"

"I had no idea he was your boyfriend. I'm sorry." There was an awkward silence. "I… I should go. It was nice talking with you, Mister Palmer."

"Likewise." There was another silence between my mom and Dad. Although I was half asleep by this point, I could feel the tension between them.

"What the fuck, George?"

"Hey, our daughter is right there! And it's not like you've ever expressed any interest in getting back together. Where were you anyway?"

"You know where! I was working!" I could hear the angry tones in their whispers.

"And our daughter has been here waiting for you! Wanting you to be here!"

"Oh well excuse me for trying to pay for her education!"

"You make that sound like a bad thing!"

"Well, if she didn't have *your* temper, we might not even be in this situation!"

"It's still no excuse to not be here for your daughter!"

"Whatever. I'm not going to sit here and take this."

"Take what?"

"Nothing. I'm leaving. My break is almost over anyway?"

"You're not going to stay for her? You realize she needs surgery, right?" What was surgery?

"Yay!" she said sarcastically. "Another bill to pay for."

"Stop it." A slap.

"Fuck you, George! You want company? Call the nurse back!"

"Jennifer! Jennifer!" I could not see, but I knew my mother was gone. She did not even stop to say hello to me.

*

I woke up in the same position I fell asleep in; curled up on one end of a sofa in my dad's personal library with a book barely finished in my lap. Looking out the window, I could see that it was still dark outside and the clock on the wall told me it was three in the morning. Something was certain though, I was hungry, and I could really use a drink. I stood up and made my way through the dark house to the kitchen, making sure to place my book face down on the page I was on to save my spot. I left the kitchen dark as I opened the fridge. The light was enough to light up the floor around me and it was almost blinding as my eyes attempted to adjust themselves. After scanning for a minute, I decided on a cheese stick and a bottle of water; more than enough to fill up someone as small as I was.

After closing the fridge, I looked up and noticed a faint glow coming from the next room. I was nervous but curious at the same time. Peeking around the corner, I saw someone sitting at a computer looking at YouTube videos. They must have sensed me, because they turned around to look at me.

"Hey, Sarah." It was Miss Melody.

"Hey," I replied sheepishly.

"What are you doing up so early?" she asked me. I shrugged my shoulders.

"I woke up in the office and wanted a drink. What about

21

you?"

"Oh, I suffer from mild insomnia." I tilted my head to the side. It was the first time I had ever heard that word.

"What's 'insomnia?'"

"It's a sleeping disorder that prevents me from sleeping properly at night."

"Okay...?" I was still confused.

"Basically, I can stay up longer than most people. For many hours."

"Like, how many?" She thought about it for a moment.

"I think the longest I stayed up was sixty-eight hours, if I remember correctly."

"Really?" I got excited. "I want insomnia! I could read so many books if I had insomnia!" She let out a light chuckle.

"You don't want insomnia, sweetheart."

"How come?"

"It comes with some nasty side effects like headaches and it makes it very hard to focus the longer I stay awake."

"Oh." I was almost disappointed.

"Don't worry. Do you want to watch some of these videos with me?"

"Sure," I replied and she pat the chair next to her.

I curled up and we began watching the videos. She showed me some weird videos with a lot of stuff moving in slow motion with two British guys talking about it and others had some animated people in armor just standing in a canyon talking. I could not remember all of them as I slowly fell asleep next to Miss Melody. I dreamed about her and Dad and I was really starting to like her too. She was like my mom, but a lot nicer. It was hard to believe she had been with my dad for two years already, but, at the same time, it felt like she belonged here.

The second time I woke up, a bright light was shining through the closed blinds of a nearby window. There was a comfort around me and I felt around to try and place myself. I was in my bedroom at Dad's house. The heavy grey comforter tucked around me was keeping me warm from the cold air that tried to come in from outside. I sat up and rubbed my eyes. On the bedside table was the book I was reading in the office last night, closed now but bookmarked on the page I left it open to. I could smell bacon and eggs as they sizzled in the pan and, for a moment, I was happy, I was at peace. It only lasted for two months.

Miss Melody was beginning to be sad all the time. I would wake up in the night and hear crying. I could always tell it was Melody. Dad was having me over less and less as it went on and, eventually, he stopped having me over at all. I loved Miss Melody, and I knew that he did too. I missed getting to see her. Living between my mom and Dad became living with just my mom and I hated it. My dad eventually came around a couple of weeks after Miss Melody became sad and he pulled me out of school early that day.

"Hey there, sweet pea." He looked tired.

"Hey, daddy." I climbed into his truck and set my bag down at my feet. "What are we doing?"

"We're going to go have a talk." He sighed before pulling away from the school.

We drove past the park and my mom's neighborhood before pulling into a local ice-cream shop. It was my favorite. They had so many different flavors that you could put together and so many toppings to pick from. The best part, some of the toppings were free of charge. However, I was curious as to why we were here. Dad usually only brought me here for celebrations, so coming here when he was upset did not make sense to me. We went inside and ordered our dessert. I had a single chocolate scoop with some cookie dough bites, but when we sat down, I hesitated to eat any of it. As far as I could see, so was he. He sighed again before he finally spoke up.

"Look, Sarah, I won't sugarcoat it. Miss Melody has been very sick lately."

"Is she going to get better?" I asked, my head tilted.

"I'm not sure but, Sarah, listen she…" but I did not listen.

"What if we made her some soup? We can take it to her at the hospital. Oh! And we can stay and spend time with her like she did for me."

"She's not going to get any better!" my dad snapped. I felt myself sink further into my chair.

"What do you mean?"

"What I mean is…" he sighed. "She's gone, Sarah. She's not going to come back." Another heavy sigh. "Not this time."

It took a while for me to understand what it was that he was saying, more like two weeks to be exact and even then, I was still a little confused. The wooden box sat at the end of the building where a cross and colored glass stood behind it. Everyone was dressed in black and the only sign of Miss Melody was her picture in a small frame with a pine wreath around it standing next to the box. She was still so pretty and there were so many people here to see her, but they were all crying. Even my dad was shedding tears at this gathering of sorts. I wanted to know what was going on but I was told that I was too young to understand. I began to wonder, is this what happens when people get really sick? Is this where they go when they do not come back?

My mother cursed my father for taking me there. Even she said I was too young. Everyone kept saying 'too young.' Too

24

young for what? I finally got home to her, and she sent me to change while she had a conversation with my dad in the living room. It was not hard to hear them. Mom said the walls in the house were thin and that she could hear most anything through them.

"What the fuck were you thinking? Taking our daughter to a funeral! Are you insane?" My mother was mad.

"I thought that she should be there because of how much of a liking she had taken to Melody." My father did not yell but simply raised his voice to get his point across.

"Oh, 'Melody' this and 'Melody' that! That's all you ever seem to talk about anymore!" She paused. "I think you took Sarah to that dreadful place simply so you wouldn't have to face that poor girl's family by yourself you coward!"

"I am no coward, and we didn't even talk to Melody's family much at all."

"Of course, you didn't, because you fear commitment!"

"This again?"

"What do you mean 'this again?'"

"Why do you always have to make it about you, Jennifer? I did this for Sarah and for my own closure and that's it."

"Oh? And who is it that allowed her to commit suicide?" A long pause.

"That was uncalled for. You know she was depressed, and I tried to talk her down every night and day. So, don't say I didn't try."

"Whatever." I could almost imagine my mother's dismissive hand wave. "Why don't you go to Hell, George? Maybe that suicidal skank will be waiting there for you." There was a silence before I heard footsteps, and the slamming of our front door. I peeked my head out to see my mother standing there by herself, red in the face and breathing hard. I did not want to pressure her, but I was curious.

"Mommy, what's suicide?" I asked. She sighed.

"It's nothing, baby. You don't need to worry yourself with it."

"Why did Miss Melody?" Again, she sighed, more irritated this time.

"Because Miss Melody was broken. And you're not, so don't worry about it."

"Why not?"

"Because I said so! Now, go get changed out of those dreadful clothes." I nodded, and walked back to my room to the sound of my mother opening the freezer and pulling out the cheap whiskey she thought I did not know about.

Evil Angel

Middle school, the land of bitches and snooty heiresses that wanted nothing more than to see me bow at their feet and bend to their will. Despite having written more papers and solved more math equations than even some of the others at the top of the academic pyramid. I guess that was why I was at the top of the academic pyramid, save for the required gym class that continued to beat me down and make me feel smaller than I already was. How it was that I had still not hit a growth spurt of any kind was beyond me, my mother, and the doctors. Girls were beginning to make more fun of me in the locker room because of it. Most of them, while we changed, would spend their time conversing about how 'big' one another had gotten in the chest and comparing sizes. It was all about who was bigger while I sat in the corner, and watched them emotionlessly feel one another up. Every now and then, they snuck peeks into my corner and laughed at me. It made my own chest feel heavy, but not in the way I wanted it to.

It did not help that people already knew me as the girl who fell off the rope a couple of years ago, which gave me a failing score for that class and a reputation as the clumsy girl on campus. Not to mention the nightmares of falling off the rope, landing on my head and snapping my neck. Granted, there were times I felt like it might be an easy way out. Every time it came to the obstacle courses, I would get a crushing feeling in my chest and my body would begin to shake. It made for some very interesting trips to the nurse's station where the only thing she could suggest was asthma, but even I could tell she was stumped with it. There was a brief moment of hope for me when we were sent to the obstacle course for our mid-semester test, and they gave us one that looked like it did not have a section with a rope or any climbing.

I changed into my gym uniform and lined up on the line to wait for the instructor. The other girls glared at me as they walked past to their spots in line. Bitches, all of them, and each one standing a head, or more, taller than me. I stayed quiet. Our instructor marched us out to the course. It was something brand new, bought by the school's massive private funding from both ROTC sponsors and university preparatory funds. Not to mention the numerous fundraisers and the amount of money funneling in from parents hellbent on wanting their kids to do well. Money in exchange for good grades, it was no wonder why keeping myself at the top of the list seemed like more of a challenge than it should have.

I looked at the new structure and felt like hurling. I could already feel my breath leaving me and my mouth going dry as I failed to prepare myself. My legs were shaking as the girls before me went. I do not want to do this. I slowly moved up in the line as I approached the obstacle. It was a set of bars that increased in height the further one crossed them until the halfway point where it dropped back down again. Each girl before me passed it with ease as they took the bars two at a time. It eventually came to my turn and, as I stepped up, I could feel everyone's eyes on me. It did not help me with my breathing, and I could feel my body turning to jelly as I tried to force myself closer to the first bar. Our coach was the first to speak up.

"Let's go, Cranston! We don't have all day!" It reminded me

of the day I fell off the rope, his screaming bringing me to scared, angry tears while I climbed.

Slowly but surely, I began working my way across the bars, but I could not take them two at a time like the others, my arms were too short. Regardless, I struggled across, but it was not easy. My breathing was failing while I exerted myself and my arms quickly became weak with fatigue. Not even halfway up the incline, my hand started slipping, and I could not get my grip back with the other. I began to panic and eventually lost my grip entirely. I reached for the bar again but missed and fell. I hit the ground with my bad arm and both heard and felt the snap.

"Shit!" I screamed painfully. Gasps echoed around me before my body was carried toward the nurse's station.

I waited for what felt like hours after my shoulder was reset. No one would say a word to me, and I was beginning to worry what it was I had done wrong. In all honesty, I knew what I did wrong. I was just hoping for the best as my heart sank. My dad was the first one who showed up and he looked more tired than usual, but he also looked upset. It made me scared, and it made me sad. My mother showed up and did not hesitate to verbally attack us both.

"What are you doing here?" she shouted at my father. "And you!" She looked at me. "What the hell were you thinking?"

"Jennifer, stop. She…"

"No, you stop! We're in this mess because you can't hold your tongue!" Silence followed by footsteps.

"Miss Cranston, Mister Palmer, Miss Sarah Jane, please come with me." It was the principal. He led us to his office and sat down behind his computer, bringing up my school record.

My father pulled a chair out for me to sit because of my arm, but my mother beat me to the seat. He offered me his, but I took the one in the corner instead. I did not want to face them while they talked. How could I listen? I knew I messed up. I knew I broke the rules; the golden rule to be exact. No profanity, zero tolerance.

"Miss Cranston, Mister Palmer, I am at a loss," my principal began. I tuned out the rest.

All I could see was my principal explaining the situation to my parents and the expressions that they held on their faces while he did. My mother's face twisted into a face of anger and disgust. Her eyebrows crossed and her teeth grinding. My father's face just dropped and his head sank. It made me sad. Instead of feeling heavy this time, my chest hurt and I could feel the lump caught in my throat. It felt like I was being squeezed. Is this what it meant to have a broken heart? Is this what it felt like for it to break?

"Unfortunately, I have no choice but to ask you to find another school for your daughter."

"There's no changing your mind?" my mother asked while leaning in closer to him. There was no doubt she was trying to use her body to persuade him. My dad sat back and rolled his eyes.

"N-no. There's no changing my mind, Miss Cranston. I'm sorry."

"Very well…" my mother stood and left without waiting for me or my father.

Dad looked at me with pity and sorrow in his eyes before standing and helping me up from my chair and leading me out, my backpack in his hand rather than on my shoulder. He was considerate. My mom was not. She was sitting in the car waiting, stepping out once she saw the two of us emerge from the front office.

"What are you doing?" We just stared at her. "She needs to be carrying her own bag."

"Jennifer, you hear the principal. She disloc…"

"I don't care. This is the second time we have had to find a school for her because of the way she wants to act, so she can carry her own bag." She was right. This was all my fault.

I took my bag by the handle and tried to throw it over the same arm I grabbed it with. My dad gave me that pitiful look again and offered to help, but I denied it. He even went to open the car door for me but a look of anger from my mom and my stubbornness led him to surrender again. I could see he wanted to help, and I wanted him to, but my mother simply would not let up. I got in the car and my dad got the door for me while I fumbled with the seatbelt single handed.

"I'll be by later to talk about schools if you want," he said. "I just have a few more things to…"

"You are not coming over!" My mother was having a field day with interrupting him. "Why not? Because I don't want you to. You've done enough, so you can stay out of this one." She started the car and aggressively pulled away from the school and from my dad with tire smoke trailing in the rearview. He did not even get to say goodbye.

My mother did not say a word to me the entire car ride home, and when I went to turn on the radio just to get some sort of sound inside, she smacked my hand away. She was pissed. I did not care anymore, I just wanted to be invisible. I felt invisible, and I sank mentally and physically into the seat of the car. My mother grabbed me by my bad shoulder and tried to pull me up.

"Sit up! We're almost home." I did as she said and winced in pain from where her thumb dug deep into the joint that was still sore from being reset.

31

When we got home, I set my bag by the door where I always sat it and tried to escape up to my room. Again, my mother grabbed my shoulder and spun me toward the kitchen table, giving me a hard shove that almost knocked me over, to make sure I obeyed. I sat down and adjusted my sling to make it a little more comfortable. She sat down opposite me and opened up her laptop. I assumed; she was looking for schools for me to go to.

"You're lucky boarding schools are expensive or else that would be my first option." She kept scrolling. "Military schools would be too easy for you because of your dad." It was hard to tell if she was talking to me or at me. Some more scrolling. If I had been honest with myself, I did not care where she sent me. Anything beat the horrors of home-schooling that I had heard of from other girls. That and I was willing to go anywhere if it meant not being at home with my mother.

She kept me there for several minutes while she scrolled through local schools, and I developed the largest migraine. It felt like my head was splitting in two and it sent pain through my arms as well as my skull. I could feel my eyes crossing as they began to blur. My sight was nearly gone until my mother shocked me back to my senses when she grabbed my shoulder for the third time. My eyes shot white with pain as it brought me back into the room.

"Here we go. There's a school not even a mile away from the house we can send you to. Why didn't I think of that? Granted we'll have to interview with them but still! It's perfect! Don't you think?" She looked at me, but all I could manage was a slow nod. My head was still killing me and her sudden outburst was not helping. "Great! I'll schedule a meeting for this next Monday." I was lost at that point. She had me on the ropes, and I just did not have the energy to say anything. I stood and went to my room without her keeping me in my seat.

Collapsing in my bed, my exhaustion caught up to me, and I was quickly felling the heaviness of my eyelids. Everything faded to black as I fell asleep, my head still splitting but with a sort of buffer. I could feel myself shaking, slipping closer to absolute darkness.

*

I was back in school, but it felt… different. A large group of people stood before me, surrounding me. All of them were so much taller than me. A rope hung in front of my face, and I was being yelled at by a commanding female voice to climb it, ring the bell. A clock starts ticking and I begin climbing. This world is a black box with no sky and no clouds. Just me, my peers, the instructor, and the rope. I keep climbing but everything hurts. I look down and it is only a black space. I look up and it is the same, but I have to keep climbing. My hand reaches up to grab higher on the rope, but the rope is gone. I am falling into the abyss and everyone is laughing out of the darkness.

I flail my arms and finally grab onto something but it is equally as terrifying. It was the bars, and I was hanging at their highest point. I swayed on them as something tried to force my grip to loosen. I could not let go. Not now, but something snapped in my rage to stay held onto the bar. It was my arm snapped in two at the elbow. Another crack and the other came off at my shoulder. Again, I was tumbling, falling and spinning through empty, black space. It took almost no time at all for the ground to finally come into view out of the darkness. The distance was closing rapidly and slowly at the same time, and I could not do anything to stop it while my face came within inches

33

from the surface.

*

I shot up in a panic. Sweat dripped down my face, and I could feel my clothes gripping to every inch of my body. My mouth was dry and I could not breathe. Shaking, I got up from my bed. It was dark outside and I could hear my mother snoring loudly in the other room. I stumbled down the hall and into the bathroom where I collapsed over the edge of the toilet. Staring into the white bowl, I felt like I was going to be sick, but I did nothing but dry heave. It brought back my headache and sent waves of pressure and pain through my chest and my shoulder.

I finally got my strength back and made my way to the mirror, and I looked like a mess. My hair was tangled and clinging to my face. I must have fallen asleep in my clothes and they were a mess too. It looked like I was hit by a bus; I felt like I was hit by a bus. Everything hurt and my body felt weak. Maybe I needed to go back to bed? I made my way to my room and lied down, but I could not sleep. Anytime I closed my eyes, the nightmares began again. Trying to get up the next morning was just as painful and the nausea continued.

I headed downstairs where my mother had made breakfast for us but the smell made me sick. What did not help was the fact that she had not actually made anything, but just heat up some frozen sandwiches she bought from the store. It reminded me of how Dad did most of the cooking. I think the last time Mom had actually cooked, she burned it. I felt like it was what I was staring at now on my plate; a failed attempt to take care of me. There was no way I could eat; I did not have the mood or the energy.

It went on like this all weekend and most of it I spent

34

between my room and the bathroom, throwing up and trying to get rid of my headache. Nothing was working. I was not eating or sleeping, and the nightmares came too easily and I was getting maybe two hours from them before waking up in a panic. One night left me scared enough to wake up in a fit of tears. It was the weekend that passed in pain and suffering up until the day of the interview with my new school.

My mother was beginning to have a pattern with K-12 schools where they sort of gave a shit. It was a larger school this time that was only recently accepting students due to being under construction for the past three years. Three buildings separated the elementary, middle, and high school students. Another stood separately across the street, and I made it out as the notorious seminary building that I had kept hearing about. The building at the front of the school said 'ADMINISTRATION' in big bold letters, while two more stood off to the side; one with a football field behind it, and the other with a roof so tall it had to be an auditorium. If I was honest with myself, it looked and felt too big to be a school, but the small hoard of students told me otherwise. We walked into the admin building where we waited for the principal to be done with whatever it was he was doing. Even in this room I felt small.

"Miss Jennifer and Miss Sarah Cranston?"

"Yes!" my mother said, standing quickly to approach the man who addressed us. I stood to face him as well. He was a taller gentleman dressed in a nice suit and tie to match the school's colors; blue, silver, and black. An odd mix of colors to me, but the mascot was a knight and the way it was designed made sense with the colors. This man also wore a pair of slim glasses that barely covered his eyes. It looked professional and they made him look smart and kind of handsome. My mother must have

35

thought so too, because she instantly started to put herself out there, pushing up her chest and undoing a couple of buttons on her shirt.

"Good morning, Mister Jefferson! I'm Jennifer, and this is my daughter, Sarah." She had that fake singsong tone to her voice.

"It is good to meet you both. I have everything set up for us in the conference room." He stuck a hand out, gesturing for us to follow. "Right this way." My mother and I followed him and she seemed almost more excited than I was to be there. Then again, I did not necessarily care what was going on.

The conference room was smaller than a normal classroom, but the table was large enough to seat maybe twenty people. It felt unfitting for a meeting with three people, but there was one other person in the room waiting already. She had long blonde hair like me and was dressed more casually than the principal was with a baseball hat and a tight ponytail. He pulled out two chairs for us and my mother took the one closest to him, leaving me sitting in front of the stranger in the room. I did not care. I was starting to get dizzy again and my head fell into my hand.

"Are you okay, sweetie?" the lady asked, taking hold of the hand I still had resting on the table. I looked at her and nodded. "You sure? You're awfully pale."

"I'm sure," I said, a bit shakily. I was not okay, but I did not feel like dealing with my mother.

The conversation they had was boring. and I tuned out most of it. Every now and then I would hear the mention of my so-called 'history of violence' as my mother called it. I think she was over exaggerating it a little bit, but the principal brought up the fact that I was not the only one involved in the fights as well as the fact that my 'bad language' was purely situational with the mentions of my injuries. I could feel the lady across from me staring at me, and I could feel the dizziness begin to have an effect on my body. The principal brought me out of my space when he closed his folder.

"Well, we've done just about everything that we can here," he said. "If you'd like, Miss Johnson can show you around the campus a little bit so you can get a feel for where your classes are going to be."

"What about you? Can't you show us the campus?" my mother asked. She still had that stupid, little, flirtatious grin on her face. The principal cleared his throat.

"I have some of my own business to attend to. I'm sorry," and before my mother could say anything else, he left the room and Miss Johnson took our attention away from him.

"We were able to get your transcripts from your previous school and we have already drawn up a schedule for your classes for the rest of the year. I'll say I'm impressed with how many of them have to be advanced-level classes. Our middle school doesn't have many of the classes you need, so we're going to go ahead and put you in some of the freshman classes." I nodded as she handed me the paper.

She escorted us out through the back toward a small cart and urged us to get in. It looked like one of those golf carts that I had seen some of the richer people drive around town to avoid walking, but it was blue instead of white and had the school's logo stuck to the front of it. It was a smooth ride as she drove us over to the high school building and the campus was really pretty. So many trees and a ton of grass. It was so green and so much better than the desert landscaping the private school had. Some landscapers were still there mowing the grass and trimming some of the bigger trees. I wished they would stop, big fluffy trees looked so much better to me. We finally pulled in front and got into the cooler air.

Blue lockers rested against grey walls with spaces between them for water fountains and doors to get into the classrooms. I liked that it was a wide hallway with not too many turns, minus the stairs in the middle of the building. Miss Johnson took us through them and told us where everything was. She mentioned that because all of my classes were freshman level, that all of my classes would be downstairs. I liked that too. All of the classes were separated by grade level so I would be working with the same peers all through school. She said it was because they 'wanted students to build lasting relationships with their peers to create a better working environment.'

We were on our way back out to the golf cart when a bell rang and students began to come out into the hallway, and there were a lot of them. The bell hurt my ears and the sudden crowding was making me nervous. I could feel my hands start to tremble as students almost twice my size began to force their way around us. We moved to the side of the hall and out of the way of traffic but it did not help. I began to see spots as my dizziness hit me, and I could feel myself swaying before everything went black.

*

I woke up with the feeling of something cool covering my forehead, and I could not tell where I was. Okay, I knew where I was. The one trip when I broke my arm left me terrified of this place. I remembered Miss Melody and how nice and caring she was. This is where I met her. At least, I thought it was the same place. I could not remember which hospital I was taken to. The

38

beeping was constant and something in my arm hurt. I looked down and saw a tube and traced it back up to the drip bag that was hanging from a silver pole. The room was quiet otherwise, and I looked around to see if anyone was here with me. No one. I saw that I was still in my normal clothes at least, and laid my head back down on the pillow and closed my eyes. My head was still pounding, and I could feel it in my ears. It did not take long for everything to subside into sleepy nothingness, but it was short lived.

"Oh. You're awake. How are you feeling?" It was Miss Johnson.

"I'm tired."

"That is to be expected." Someone else walked into the room with another drip bag. She was dressed in all blue.

"Where's my mom? Where's my dad?" The two exchanged glances.

"Sarah, what do you remember from the last couple of days?" I had to think. What did I remember?

I remembered the interview and the tour, and I remembered not feeling good. The weekend was not all that great, I think. I remembered nightmares and not eating, but I did not want to talk to them about that. Did I? I did not know anymore. Instead, I sat there and stared at her. Her eyes looked curious, but I could not look at them. I could feel myself shaking, and I looked away from her and started staring at the wall. Why did I feel so alone?

"Sarah," she put a hand over mine and sat down next to me on the bed. "You can tell me." I shook my head as my lip began to shake, and I closed my eyes. "Okay." She stood and left me in the room by myself again.

Why am I so helpless? Why could I not tell her how I was feeling? I trusted her, right? She was talking to someone in the

39

hall but I did not know who.

"Are you sure?"

"I haven't been able to get a hold of her mother for hours now. Her father answered but he's out of town and unable to make it out here."

"Very well. We'll keep trying her mother. Until then, she'll have to stay here."

Their voices faded and left me completely alone as their footsteps echoed down the hall and away from my room. Despite all of the lights in the room, I felt like I was sitting in the dark. I pulled my knees to my chest and hugged them as tight as I could. It still was not enough. I closed my eyes. I needed someone here with me. I wanted someone here with me. Where did everybody go?

Dear Agony

The words danced off the page of the literature test that sat in front of me as phrases from Shakespeare's *Hamlet, Romeo and Juliet,* and *Julius Caesar* failed to enter my mind right when I needed them most with little time left. It was not like me to have issues like this and it was starting to piss me off. When in doubt answer 'C.' At least, that is what I thought everyone always said. How would I know? No one would talk to me, and it was sometimes better that way. The familiar pressure of the black stress ball I kept with me during these kinds of tests rested in my clenched fist that I opened and closed to match the rhythm of my breathing. It felt softer than normal, and I struggled to keep my focus on the test because of it. My eyes scanned the paper. Still nothing. This was the worst. Why could I not focus?

The school bell finally signaled the end of class, and my teacher went around collecting all the tests. I frantically scribbled down some more answers before she took mine. I felt ashamed. This was the first test I failed to finish since I started attending. Honestly, it was the first test I failed to finish, ever. My teacher looked at me with an air of concern in her face and it made me panic. Embarrassed, I collected my things and left her class. I hugged my books close to my chest as I flew through the hallway past the mob of students. It was a free period for me and I went to the only place I felt comfortable; the library. Other students in their free period were scrambling to the tutoring centers and left the place empty, except for Miss Levey who was busy stacking books on their proper shelves.

I looked around the room and found a spot to place myself near the window. The sun was peeking through the slats sending streaks of light across the wood table. I should have pulled out my books and started studying for my next class, but I could not find it in me to move my bag from the floor. Instead, I looked through the slats and out the window into the courtyard at the center of campus. My dad would have been furious with me. He always had high hopes for me and wanted me to do my absolute best no matter what. It was embarrassing to know that I did not finish that test, even if it was the first for me. Thinking back, I could not even remember how many questions were on it or even how many questions I had answered before the end of class. Oh god, what was my mother going to say? The only reason they let me into this school was because of my test scores and my untarnished record, save for the fights and suspensions from unfortunate circumstances. She would have my head on a silver platter if she had to go looking for another school for me. No, I could not let that happen. I did not need another beating from her.

"Are you okay, sweetie?" My eyes shot up from the table and made contact with Miss Levey.

"Yeah, I'm fine," I lied. I was screaming on the inside. She gave me a worried look.

"Okay, just let me know if you need anything." She walked away with her now empty book cart behind her. I continued to sit there and stare into space.

The lines in the table started to melt into a single blob of color. I could feel my eyes begin to burn but I could not find it in me to blink the moisture back into them. Instead, I continued to let them dry out. It made me wonder what it was that helped keep the eyes moist. Was it the same liquid that helped my joints or was it something else like a mucus from the brain? I should have made a note to ask my biology teacher the next time I saw her.

A hand touched my shoulder startling me. I looked up, and it was my counselor, Miss Johnson. She was always so nice to me and reminded me of Miss Melody sometimes. I missed her too, and dad. He did not come around as much anymore, not since she died. Miss Johnson's eyes looked concerned for me, and I could tell she was trying to read the emotions on my face. She looked at me the same way Miss Levey did. I was starting to think she called her down here.

"Come on," Miss Johnson said, nodding her head toward the door of the library that led out and toward the counselor's office in the administration building.

Several students glanced at me as I walked through the halls with her. I made eye contact with a couple of them and the looks they gave me sent nervous chills down my spine. A few of them were going back to their groups and gossiping all the while keeping their eyes on me. Well, most of them were; enough that it felt like all of them. I put my head down and kept walking, the lockers blurring past me. Regardless, I could still feel their eyes on me. I hated it. Every bit of it. I knew what happened when people saw you in the hallways with anyone from admin. The stories I heard them talk about others were ones I did not want to be known for. The number of girls labelled as sluts and shamed and outcasts because of an assumption. It is not like I did not have enough of that already. The facts of my life that I kept to myself caused them to assume my life story was already the nightmare that I was living day to day. We finally reached her office and she motioned for me to sit down. Finally, the feeling of everyone's eyes went away, and I felt relatively normal. All I needed was to keep taking deep breaths and everything would be okay. At least I hoped.

"I'll be right back." Miss Johnson left me alone in her office. I tried to catch a glimpse of her as she left to see where she was going, but the way her door was positioned, I could not see past the wall that separated the counsellors from the rest of the administrators.

My heart started to feel like it was going to spring from my chest, and I could not breathe. Why did it feel so warm and why was I there anyway? Every question that crossed my mind made my heart beat faster and my breathing more ragged and broken. What was going on? Miss Johnson eventually returned with my English teacher who was holding onto something that made me curious. It was a packet of some sort. She sat next to me while Miss Johnson took her seat opposite us by her computer. She started typing something in, and all of a sudden, my grades were sitting there on the screen staring me in the face. It felt like an academic status report meeting, but the next report was more than a month away with my half semester report still sitting in my backpack from the other day. Miss Johnson finally got herself situated and turned to look at me.

"Are you doing okay, Sarah?" Her question was genuine but still made me anxious to answer.

"I'm fine," I lied.

"Miss Levey said you weren't acting like yourself today, and when I asked Miss Anderson here, she says she noticed the same thing."

"I am fine, really." I let out a nervous laugh and let my eyes wander down into my lap. I began scratching at the pit between my thumb and index finger. It was already red and raw, but I did not feel it.

"Sarah," Miss Anderson put a hand over mine. "If you want,

44

I can let you retake this test. I know this is not normal of you and I know you are capable of acing it without breaking a sweat."

"Thank you," I mumbled. I could hear my voice and it sounded weak. It disgusted me.

"Thank you, Miss Anderson," Miss Johnson said, letting my English teacher leave the two of us alone in her office. "Sarah, I can help you with whatever it is that's going on. You don't have to fight against it alone, and I can find you someone that can help explain what it is that's affecting your mind." I thought about it but everything in my brain was telling me not to while my heart told me to accept her offer, but my heart was what always got me hurt.

"My mom won't know, will she?" I looked at her and she seemed surprised. The idea of my mother knowing about meeting with my counselor or knowing that they thought there was something wrong in my head made me shiver. The way she expressed herself in times of my health was nothing glamorous. Not to mention my first time here, she tried flirting with the already married principal, whose daughter was is in my PE class and made fun of me for it.

"We don't have to tell her if you don't want to," she said, which eased my nerves.

"Thank you." She put a hand on mine.

"I can bring someone in if you would like to talk to them." I shook my head.

"I would rather just talk to you," I said. She nodded in understanding.

"Okay. Do you want to start now? We can get you excused for your classes today."

"Sure." Miss Johnson began typing on her computer again before pulling out a notepad and setting it on her desk.

45

"So," she began, "what do you want to talk about?"

I let everything out. I told her about how my mother had been treating me and ignoring me when I needed her. I told her about all of the days I woke up in sweat from the recurring nightmares. I even told her about how no matter how much I tried, I could not will myself to find joy in anything. Not even my favorite books could help bring me to focus on anything. My mind was constantly wandering and even while we talked, I had a hard time struggling to focus.

"When was the last time you saw your dad?" Miss Johnson asked me. I shrugged.

"He doesn't come around much anymore. Mom says it's because he doesn't love me and doesn't care about me, but when he does come over, Mom is always yelling at him."

"Does she yell at you?"

"Not really." I had to think about it for a moment. "She usually just sighs angrily and walks away. That, and she doesn't really ever ask me how I'm doing." Miss Johnson nodded and continued to write a couple of things down in her notebook. The final bell for school rang and Miss Johnson looked down at her watch.

"Well, look at that." She closed the book and smiled at me. "Thank you for coming to talk to me, Sarah," I nodded. "Is there anything else you want to get off your chest?" I shook my head. I did not know what to say. "Okay, sweetie. Well, just remember, I am always here to talk." Again, I nodded, then picked up my bag and went to leave her office. "Have a good weekend!" she called to me, but I did not respond.

I walked home alone like I always did and my mind continued to wander, only coming out of my random thoughts to stop and wait at the stop lights. Cars sped through the

46

intersections, and I tried to count each one as it went by while also trying to note the color and the brand of the car. It was one of the few things that helped me focus on anything, but when I did, it was the only thing I could focus on.

The little white person told me to go ahead, and I began to cross the busy street. A loud horn and a screech echoed in my ears, and I was quickly pulled back as a black truck sped through the corner. My heart was pounding in my ears and my breath in my chest. I turned around to look at the person who pulled me back and my eyes fell upon another girl with long black hair and dressed in a black skirt and top. I locked onto her eyes as she did with mine and I felt like my stomach had grown lighter.

"Are you okay?" she asked. I nodded, unable to speak. What I was going to say quickly flew into my mind but I struggled to get it out.

"Thank... you..." I stammered.

"You're welcome," she replied.

I stood there speechless and unable to move. Her eyes were so blue. So many thoughts were running through my mind that I was having a hard time remembering what I was doing. She was looking at me too and I could feel the butterflies in my stomach. A nervous laugh and a smile left her lips.

"Are you sure you're okay...?" I blinked a few times, bringing me back to the moment before answering.

"Yeah... sorry..." I could not believe I spaced out there. She giggled and extended a hand.

"I'm Andrea, by the way."

I took her hand and could feel my own shaking. "Sarah..." I managed to get out.

*

47

I walked in the front door and set my backpack down on the table in the entryway. I kicked off my shoes and slid them underneath it and made my way into the kitchen. My mother was standing at the counter with a glass in hand that held an odd colored liquid. A bottle with the same liquid sat on the counter near her with the word 'Jack' printed in bold white letters on a black label.

"Where the fuck have you been?" she slurred. A hiccup left her lips.

"I took a small detour through the library." Not a complete lie but it was.

"Whatever." She waved a dismissive hand at me and walked over to the kitchen table where she laid her head down in her arms. Within seconds, she was snoring.

I escaped up the stairs into the bathroom where two bright orange-colored bottles were waiting for me. On the labels read 'Clonazepam' and 'Sertraline Hydrochloride.' *Half doses until we can figure out what's going on, then we'll adjust them accordingly.* Those were the instructions the doctors had given me. I wish they were helping, but my mother was not. My dad was the one who took me to the psychiatrist as requested by my doctor after she noted that I had an abnormal heart rate. I took the half doses and swallowed them down with a full glass of water. The pills left a chalkiness in my mouth that I thought only my mother's cooking could do. The effects took over and I could feel my heartbeat slowing down and my mind start to clear up. I went to my room and laid down in my bed, letting the clearness of my mind take over. They drifted to the black-haired girl I saw earlier in the day. She was so pretty and her body had a perfect shape. Why was I thinking about her?

Daylight

I stumbled into the locker room, my legs felt like bowls of jelly, numb and limp. My gym locker was sitting on the other side of the room, but felt like the other side of the campus, maybe even the other side of town. Wobbling and feeling my way along the wall, I had to fight to keep upright as the other girls rushed into the locker room to change for their next class. I tripped over my own foot and almost landed face first on the concrete floor, but stopped by the girl behind me when she grabbed me under the arm and pulled me up. She was a little taller than me, and I felt like I was being lifted off my feet instead of helped to them. We moved slowly through the throng of girls until we reached the benches where she finally set me down. She moved in front of me and leaned against the lockers, staring down at me. She was blonde like me, but the sides of her head were shaved and her hair grown out the back and tied into a single ponytail. She tossed me the water bottle she had in hand and gestured for me to drink. I took a couple sips before handing it back to her.

"Thanks," I said sheepishly.

"No problem!" she chimed. "Are you doing, okay?"

"Yeah, I'll be all right," I said with a slight gasp.

"Good!" She was almost too enthusiastic. "I hope you keep that pace the next time we run our miles. I've never had another girl push me like that before. You should try out for the track team!"

"No," I said, shaking my head. "I'm just here to run my

laps." She looked at me quizzically.

"Then where did you learn to run like that?"

"Prep school." I shrugged. "Forced us to do obstacle courses all the time."

"No shit," she murmured. "A prep school girl like you, all skin and bone with no height, almost able to outrun the fastest girl on the whole campus, and she doesn't do sports?"

"Nope." Again, I shook my head at her. She chuckled at me then leaned forward with an outstretched hand.

"Samantha Jones, but my friends call me Sam."

"Sarah Cranston." I took her hand and she gave it a hearty shake. The bell rang to signal the end of class.

"I'll see you around, Cranston." She gave me a heavy pat on the shoulder and disappeared around the corner toward the other rows of lockers.

I smiled and started changing out of my gym clothes with most of the locker room cleared out. It was almost a mad dash as I sped changed then power walked my way across campus to my next class before lunch. I jumped in the closing door just as the bell rang for class to start. The teacher looked up from the lesson plan she had in front of her on the podium while I breathlessly sucked air in through my teeth.

"Nearly late…" she said deadpan.

"Sorry," I gasped. "Just came from gym."

"Don't care. Sit down and take out your book and try not to sweat too much on my floor."

I nodded and made my way to the front of the classroom where the only open seat was with several of my classmates snickering in the background. The book, *Wuthering Heights*, a classic, and one whose cloth bound I wanted and eyed at the bookstore for months now. I had read it once before and it quickly became one of my favorites alongside *Frankenstein* and *Dracula*. I opened it up to the last page I had taken notes on and looked up to my teacher standing in front of my desk.

"Algebra, Miss Cranston." I looked up at the board and saw the equations as well as the daily warm up problem.

A heat rose in my face while the rest of the class laughed openly this time. My foot began nervously tapping while I swapped to my textbook and pulled out my assignment notebook to work on the daily problem. A balled paper hit the back of my head and I ignored it until another landed in front of me on the desk. I picked it up and opened it to big bold letters that said 'dumbass' across the length of the page from corner to corner. The paper got angrily crumpled back up and shoved into my backpack while the stinging in my eyes grew. I worked through the figures and kept my head down during the lesson looking up only to take notes that the teacher wrote up on the board.

At lunch, I stayed on the far end of the room in the corner where nobody liked to sit. It was a dark corner with a light that they refused to fix after several weeks of knowing that it was broken. The Caesar salad was the only thing not covered in grease, and what I ate every day at lunch. It was a miracle I managed to collect enough loose change around the house in order to afford it. One of the nicknames the girls gave me in gym was 'Quarters' and it sucked that so many of them knew. A tray plopped down beside me and made me jump enough to look up from the book I was reading. No one ever came over here to sit with me, and now I had a tuft of blonde hair with shaved sides sitting next to me.

"Whatcha reading, legs?" I stared at her, still dumbfounded, and confused. Instead of telling her, I lifted the book to show her the front cover. "*The Outsiders* huh?"

"You ever read it before?" I had a moment of hope for what may be a new acquaintance.

"Nope!" she chimed. "But I've seen this kick ass movie with the same name!"

"It's not bad. Still inaccurate though. *Very* inaccurate."

"How so?" She took a french-fry off her plate and popped it in her mouth.

I gave out a light chuckle. "I don't have enough time to give you a breakdown of the movie and the book."

"Then how about this weekend at my place? I can write the address down for you." She ripped a piece off her napkin and started writing it down.

"I'm not sure I would be able to, Samantha."

"You, my friend, can call me Sam. And why not?"

"My mother."

"Strict?"

"Sure," I scoffed. "Let's go with that." She had no idea.

"I get it," she continued. "My mom *loves* her Tennessee Fire."

"Huh?" Of all the bottles my mother kept, I never saw anything with that label.

"Cinnamon whiskey. She loves it. Has three bottles in the house at any given time."

"And I thought my mother was bad…" I looked down and picked a little at my salad.

"How about this?" she began again. "My sister is in town this weekend to visit with her bigshot husband. They want to take me out to the mall, why not join us?"

I thought about it. Most days I would avoid my mother to go out to the library anyway. Half the time, she was out with her new boyfriend or fiancé or whatever he was, and was usually out

52

half the night anyway. One day out at the mall would be nothing and she would not even notice if I was out longer than a couple of hours. I took the napkin Sam had written her address on and flipped it over to write my own as well as my cell number and handed it back to her. She looked at it and gave me an outrageous open-mouthed smile.

"Oh, Sarah! You, naughty girl!" she sang. "Handing out your contact info to a complete stranger! I thought you would be better than that."

"Well," I began with a shrug. "It's not my fault you consider me a friend."

"And what, my dear, gave you that impression?" She sipped deviously at her soda.

"Only your friends call you Sam," I replied. She gave me a huge smile then threw an arm around my shoulders to pull me in tight.

"Hell, yeah they do!" she said and we kept laughing together in our lonely, dimly lit corner.

*

The car that pulled up had to be the nicest one I had ever seen and definitely a step up from my mother's car that looked like something that crawled out of the late nineties or early two thousands. Brand new, jet black, with smooth leather interior. Sam's sister definitely had good taste in cars, or at least her sister's husband did. When I climbed into the back, I was instantly hit with that new car smell. It almost made me dizzy compared to the smell of my mother's car that had grown into a musky odor.

"So," her sister began. "How do you two know one other?"

53

"Met her at school earlier this week," Sam chimed. "Looked like she could use a friend."

"Well, that's nice. What's your name stranger?" Her accent sounded like she was from the south.

"Sarah," I said sheepishly. They still made me a little nervous, and I felt awkward being in their car having never met them before. Everything I was taught told me not to go with them at all and to get out of the car then, even though we were already moving away from my house.

"Well, Miss Sarah, are you sure you want to be associating yourself with my little sister here? She has quite the rap sheet and a bit of a reputation in our house." It was a tease to her younger sister, and she earned a small slug in the shoulder for it from Sam, but the two laughed it off and it turned into a small slap fight.

"Not while I'm driving, please?" her husband said with a chuckle.

"Well," I began. "Anyone willing to come sit at the loner table with me seems like they deserve a chance with my friendship." The two of them finally settled down.

"What makes you say that?" she asked.

"People never take the time with me. Most see me, they see how small I am, and just write me off as another loser. Not to mention this is my third school in two years, almost. So, it gets a little hard making friends."

She looked at me, then Sam, and then her husband. The smile on her face faded and took on a look that resembled more pity. It was a moment before she spoke again.

"Well," she said. "I guess it looks like we're your new friends then!"

"Absolutely," her husband chimed. He was very soft spoken and had a warm demeanor around him. I had to bet that he never raised his voice at all. He almost reminded me of my dad, at least when he still came around.

The drive to the mall after our introductions was full of laughter and singing while Sam and her sister started with terrible covers of Katy Perry. As much as I liked her music, I could not help but enjoy their train wreck of a performance. I caught myself wanting to hum along to some of the songs that they had playing on the radio and tried not to sing with them when my favorites came on. It was the most fun I had since I could remember and with people that did not seem like they were falling off the wagon.

In the mall, Sam made an effort to drag me into almost every girly store she could find along the first floor and even forced me into a dress that she thought would look good on me. A blue off the shoulder dress that was pencil thin in the legs and barely went down to my knees. Easy enough to get in and out of with the side zipper but still falling out of it because I had nothing to fill it out in the chest. I pulled back the curtain on the dressing room and came out holding it on like a toddler who just found their mother's nice clothes.

"What even is the point of this?" I grumbled as I hobbled out to the mirror, afraid to rip the skirt if I took too big of a step.

"Because it's fun!" Sam nearly shouted. Several other girls turned to look at us with her booming voice and I felt the heat rising in my face from embarrassment. "And because you look as cute as a button!"

I finally looked up in the mirror and almost had to agree with her. The dress was very cute and also very slimming. Not that there was much to make look slim being just over five foot and only a hundred pounds. I could have done without the color but it looked good against my skin and was a shade that almost

55

perfectly matched my eyes. It did feel weird being barefoot on the carpet in the store.

"Come on then!" Sam exclaimed. "Give me a spin!"

I looked at her with a raised eyebrow. "If I give you a spin, I'm going to fall flat on my face."

"Fine!" she sighed. "You're no fun!"

"I'm also not going to fall in a dress I don't own."

"Fair point," she said. She began looking around the room at some of the others then walked up and put her head next to mine. "I don't want to alarm you, but there is a super-hot guy that has not taken his eyes off of you since you walked out."

"Oh, please! He's probably wondering why a fourteen-year-old who looks like a ten-year-old is trying on such a nice dress."

"I don't know, his smile is telling me a very different story." I looked over my shoulder in the same direction she was, and saw the guy she was talking about.

Sitting on one of the stores' benches was a guy who I thought was very handsome. Long dark hair and bright green eyes that could be picked out among a crowd. The grin he wore told me he definitely liked what he saw, but it was not a grin on a face that made me blush at all. Instead, I felt like hiding from him. I felt more embarrassed than anything, especially when the girl he was with came out of her dressing room, failing to get his attention from me. I knew how to read him, and I did not like him.

"He's not worth it," I mumbled, and I walked back into the dressing room to change back into my jeans and my T-shirt. When I came out, he was gone.

"Hungry?" Sam asked.

"Starving!"

Sam threw an arm around me and we walked out of the store and toward the food court where we found her sister waiting for

56

us. They had gotten a pizza from one of the food stalls nearby, first time I had pizza in a long while. Pizza was always one of those that I was tempted to get for lunch at school, but after the rubber pizza incident, I could never bring myself to do it again. This pizza was good pizza and we all sat around enjoying it. It felt weird though, sitting around and getting along like a happy family. At least, it felt like we were a happy family.

On the way home, Sam pulled out a bag that she had tucked away in the bag she was carrying through the mall. It had the emblem of one of the jewelry shops we passed by. She fumbled around with it for a while before she finally got what she was fishing for out and showed it to me with a full stretched arm. It was a silver necklace, but the design on the end looked unfinished. Looking closer, I saw it was unfinished. Yin and Yang was supposed to be two curved teardrops, a black and a white, not just one white.

"I think you bought a broken one," I said. She shook her head then pulled out a silver necklace with the black teardrop.

"A matching set," she said with the biggest smile. "They interlock. One for me, and one for you. Friendship necklaces." She reached back across the car to me, gesturing for me to take it. "Well, try it on."

I took the necklace from her hands and clasped it around my neck. It hung just below my collarbone and was cold against my skin.

"Why?" I asked.

"Because you and I are a lot alike," she said with a sigh. "To be honest, I used to sit by myself a lot in school because all of the other girls were scared of me." She looked at me with a sad smile. "They used to think I wasn't human, looked like I wasn't human. They acted like I was the Incredible Hulk after he destroyed the

57

city."

"It can't be that bad, right?" I looked at her sister in the front seat, and she looked down in her lap with a frown.

"I may have dropped my mother through a table during a school function. She was drunk and making a scene so, I made an example of it and destroyed any sense of humanity that I may have had in their eyes." Sam sighed. "You're the realest friend I have ever had. Even if I have only known you for a couple of days."

"I'm sure you've had other friends."

"None like you." There was a tear in her eye. "You're the first one who has never seen me as a freak."

It hit me like a ton of bricks. There were years where I felt the same way, especially when I was attending private school. Those girls were practically all heiresses to their expensive empires they called households. Their dads always picked them up in fancy luxury cars whereas I got to either walk home or get picked up in my mother's 'lemon' as they called it. They never liked me, and thought I was a freak for not being able to live up to their expectations rather than the school's. It was like being the poor girl at rich camp. I *was* the poor girl at rich camp living day by day with a partial scholarship that only existed, because I outscored them all academically.

"You don't think I'm a freak, right?" I looked at her and she was looking down at her lap, tears in her eyes. I reached across the back seat and took her hand in mine.

"Never," I said. She smiled at me, one of the biggest smiles I have seen her wear since meeting her.

When they dropped me off, the sun was starting to set and the sky was full of hues of red and pink that receded into the purples and dark blues of night. I always liked sunset. Especially when it was cloudy. They were always so pretty.

"See you later, legs!" Sam shouted. She was practically hanging out of the window to wave goodbye.

"See you!" I shouted back, giving her a wave. I watched them pull away until I could not see their car anymore.

My mother's car was in the driveway, which meant she must have been home. A smell hit me as I approached the door. I could not recognize it, and it only got worse the closer I got. When I opened the door, I was hit in the face by a wall of smoke and saw both my mother and her boyfriend sitting on the couch with their heads hanging back and staring at the ceiling. They were going back and forth describing the shapes they saw in the popcorn patterns. I rushed to get the living room fan and the stove fan running on full blast then ran to the back door and swung it open. The smell almost seemed to be getting worse. My mother looked down from the ceiling and smiled at me, her eyes bloodshot, and uttered something completely incoherent. I could not make it out and was about to ask her to repeat herself before her head collapsed back again in a fit of wheezing laughter. I scoffed and went upstairs to my room and locked the door behind me. Sleep came easy, and I never heard my mother come upstairs for bed.

I woke up the next morning on my own, instead of to my mother's screaming voice like usual. Wiping the crud from my eyes, I made my way downstairs to make some breakfast for myself. Mom never cooked breakfast on her days off, and I never saw her eat anything in the mornings anyway. I hit the bottom step and saw my mom passed out on the couch with her head still hanging over the back looking toward the ceiling. Two fingers to her neck just below her jaw told me she was still there. I nodded and went into the kitchen.

After a few hours of reading alone in my room, my mother

finally came in. I looked up from my book to find her staring at me with a blank expression. Her hair was a mess and her clothes were tattered. I was hoping she would be sober, but she had already grabbed one of her bottles and had it hanging in her grasp. She brought it to her lips and took a long swig, her eyes never breaking contact with mine.

"What happened yesterday?" she asked almost accusingly.

"I don't know, I wasn't home," I said.

"Exactly! What happened to you yesterday?" Her words were slurring and her temper was shrinking.

"I was with a friend." I put my eyes back on the page of my book.

"Bull shit!" she barked. "I know damn well you don't have any friends!" I heard her stomp across the room toward me. She ripped my book from my hands and threw it against the wall. "Where the hell were you?" she screamed.

"Out. You weren't home anyway!" She smacked me.

"Fuck you! Lying little bitch! How dare you?"

I sprung up from my bed and pushed her at her shoulders. She went over and hit the floor like a bag of bricks, but she was still fighting and stumbling trying to trip me. I barely managed to step over her arms. My shoes were still sitting by the door, and I grabbed them as I ran out, but did not put them on as I broke into a run outside. The sidewalk was warm against my bare feet as my heels slapped against the concrete all the way down to the park where I sat on the swings by myself.

I let my toes dig into the warm sand while I rubbed the spot on my cheek that was still warm from my mother slapping me. It stung, and the more I rubbed at it, the worse it felt, but I could not find it in me to stop. She occasionally hit me when she was sober, but she always hit me when she was drinking. I was always doing something wrong and was never good enough for her. That was how I ended up spending so much time alone. The tears kept coming even after I heard the rattle of chains next to me.

"You too, huh?" I knew the voice and looked up to see Sam sitting next to me. "You all right, legs?" I nodded. "Nice looking hand print she left for you. Mine got me as soon as my sister left." Sam turned slightly to show me the dark purple bruise that circled her eye.

"Jesus…" I whispered. "How hard did she hit you?"

"She didn't hit me," she said, shaking her head. "Threw me hard enough to go flipping over the couch though. Caught my eye on the edge of the coffee table. Thank God it's got rounded corners instead of sharp ones." I reached up and cupped her cheek.

"I'm sorry you have to live with that."

"What, this?" She pointed to her eye. "This is a once-a-week regularity. Woman drinks so much Tennessee Fire she just loses it. Doesn't help any that I look just like my dad and share his last name either."

"I have my mother's last name. My dad's name is Palmer."

"That makes your name…"

"Sarah Jane Cranston. I hate it." I looked back to the sand.

"I wish it was your dad's name. Sarah Jane Palmer sounds much cooler. It sounds like a badass Marine name!" I looked over and saw her shoot straight up in the swing as she emphasized the whole motion of it. "Sergeant Sarah Jane Palmer! Top of her class! I can see it now."

"Oh, shut up!" I laughed and gave her a nudge with my shoulder. She nudged me back.

"Don't worry, legs. No matter how many dark shiners your mother gives you, or how many mine gives me, we've got one

61

another. Deal?" She held out her hand to me.

"Deal!" I said.

I pulled the white half of the yin-yang from under my shirt and held it out to her. She stood up and fished out the black half and held it close to mine. As the two pieces got close, they pulled on one another and snapped together to form their seamless circle. Linked together by magnets, just like Sam and I.

Pain

I do not remember exactly when the abuse started. What I do remember is that it came from someone I barely knew who I met about a month before my sophomore year. My mother came home late after a night out. Anxiety attacks and nightmares made me sleepless, and I watched as she stumbled drunkenly through the door. Not something I found uncommon; I was starting to think she drank to forget. This time, there was a man she had herself leaning against. His white stained shirt was half untucked, and his beard and hair looked dirty and unwashed.

They stumbled in together and she set him down on the couch near the center. He swayed as he stared at me, and I made movements to try and push myself as far into the arm and away from him as possible. I turned back to my book, still cautious of the new stranger in my house. He flopped face first into my lap and started laughing. I was terrified, nearly speechless as a startled squeal got caught in my throat.

"Umm... Mom?"

"Don't worry, Sarah," she slurs. He's just had... a bit too much to drink." She managed to get the last bit out amongst a burp that sounded too much like it wanted to come up her throat.

His laugh sent uncomfortable vibrations through my legs and into a place that only got touched in the shower. I squirmed, trying to peel him off, but he was too heavy. My mother finally came back from wherever it was she went and was able to coax the drunken man off of me and into her unstable form. Together, they swayed up the stairs. My first impression of him was not great, and I was silently scorning my mother for bringing him home.

Later that night, I found myself, yet again sleepless and brought on the verge of insanity by the noises coming from my mother's bedroom. It was the cries that carried through the hallway. It was the slamming of the headboard vibrating in the walls. It was the creaking of her bedframe echoing in my ears. It was the bane of my existence, and it went on for what felt like hours.

I got up reluctantly the next morning. My body ached from the lack of sleep and my head was spinning. Sitting up, I stretched my arms out, feeling each pop and snap that came from my chest and back. A quick shower had me mildly rejuvenated, but a glance down at my meds had me sluggish once again. *Happy Pills* are what I've heard them referred to as too many times in school. It did not make them any more bearable. I popped the lids off both bottles and swallowed them down, one each, with small handfuls of water. They were tacky and made my mouth dry regardless of how much water I chugged.

I made my way downstairs and into an empty first floor and guessed they were still asleep. I made sure to leave a note, telling my mother I was going out. It was going to be a long day trying to get myself into a normal state of mind. Only one place I can do that, the school library; luckily kept open for students who wanted to do some summer reading. One of the perks of being the only student interested. It was the only uninterrupted silence and seclusion I ever got, save for the librarian, but I actually liked her.

I opened the door and walked into the sweet aroma of fresh leather-bound books as they sat there on the cart yet to be placed on their respective shelves. It was about time too. Miss Levey and her aid had been reorganizing the shelves in the prior year in order to have room for the loaned books. I ran my hand across them on the book cart. The leather was soft, and the pages were leafed in gold and silver that glistened in the fluorescent lighting. Faint footsteps came from behind the desk.

"Good morning, Sarah."

"Good morning, Ms. Levey."

"Here for some more summer reading?" She set down another box of books on the desk near the cart.

"Of course," I chimed. "I'm eyeballing these new books, you've got here."

"Well, I was planning on putting them on the shelves today," she said with a chuckle. She started pulling at the tape that held the box closed. "But I guess I can let you be the first to read them before they go up. You know where they're going and in what order?"

"I should hope so. We didn't reorganize the whole library for no reason."

"Yeah, I guess you're right." She picked a book out of the box. It had dark red binding and black leafed pages. "This one is a classic, *and* a personal favorite." She handed it to me, and I reviewed the cover; Bram Stoker's *Dracula*.

"Thank you." I took the book over to my normal chair by the street side window. I sat there for hours reading through the pages.

Every now and again, I would glance up from the book to Miss Levey, the stack of boxes in the corner shrinking each time as she seemed to fly around the library with her cart. At one point, she brought me a glass of water and a granola bar. She was good about keeping snacks with her at all times, knowing how obsessed I would get with my books. I could sit there and read for hours without eating or drinking anything. People would tell me that I had a problem, but I was the one who excelled in my classes because of it. Miss Levey would tell me about when she had the same problem when she was my age. It was another reason she kept food in her bag or on her person at all times. I remember seeing her as she randomly pulled out a protein bar from her pocket while putting the returned books back in their places.

I finished the last page of the book and set it down on the table in front of me, observing it from the cover. It was not a dark red binding, but more resembling blood red binding. Fitting for the story. Not a story you would think of if someone told you it was a book about vampires. One of the reasons I refused to read more modern vampire stories. They were watered down and made to fit the minds of a typical teenager. Teen romances made me sick. I stood up and walked the book over to its shelf with the rest of the leather bounds.

"Did you like it?" I turned to see Miss Levey with her cart. She was finishing up with the last box of books.

"Yeah. I thought it was interesting the way it was written." I placed it in its spot. A perfect fit.

"A lot of gothic works were written like that back then," she said. "It's a shame people don't write like that anymore." I nodded.

"Any other suggestions?" I asked. Miss Levey put a hand on her chin and scanned the shelves in front of her.

"That's a hard one. There's not too much here you haven't read I don't think." Her hand started tracing over the tops of the spines and stopped on one that I had always wanted to read, but prioritized others ahead of it. "This one is good. It's no *Dracula*, but I think you'll like it." She pulled it off the shelf and handed it to me, *The Picture of Dorian Grey.*

"Thank you." I took the book in my arms and headed toward the door. "I'll see you soon!" I called.

"I don't doubt it!" she said.

*

I finally got home later that afternoon as the sun was setting behind the other houses. Once I was up the front steps, I heard what sounded like moaning coming from inside. I walked in the front door to a sight I felt I was never supposed to see. There, facing me from the living room, was my mother's chest being grabbed by large hairy hands as she screamed his name. I felt like I was going to hurl at the sight and hid behind the binding of my book while trying to make my way upstairs to my room. I slammed the door and almost threw the book onto my nightstand before burying my face in my pillow trying to remove the sounds coming from below. I was cursed with having images to go with the noises that flowed through the house at night.

Some time went by before there came a knock at my door. I stayed glued to my place. I knew who it was. I just did not want to talk to her. Another knock followed by the turn of the knob and the creaking the door made as it swung slowly open. Her footsteps were soft against the carpet.

"Hey, Sarah. Do you have a moment to talk to me?"

"Go away." I turned toward the window and away from her. She tried to lay a hand on my shoulder but I shrugged it away.

"Please, Sarah. We need to talk."

"And I don't want to. Now leave!"

"Sarah…"

"I said 'leave!'" I shouted at her. I have never shouted at her before and the person I felt did not feel like myself. I just wanted her gone.

"Very well," she said, and she slipped away silently from my room, making sure to close the door behind her. It was confirmed by the soft click of the latch. Moments later, I could hear my mother sobbing in the next room. Give me a break, like she ever cared.

There was a peaceful silence that night, and I was able to go to sleep without the gross images of my mother and her *lover* doing what they did best when they thought I was absent or asleep. I was finally going to get some peace of mind, until I heard the creaking of my door once again. It opened slowly, and it woke me in a frightened state. I could not move. I refused to move. My lungs failed me and it did not help that I was not facing the door. Instead, I was facing toward the window.

A weight presented itself behind me on my bed and pulled my blanket tight around my body. Now I was not only still from fear, but the blanket restricted my movements. I was pulled hard by my shoulder so that I was on my back, the weight now digging into my chest. One hand felt up my chest while the other was pressed against my mouth, keeping my screams from escaping my lips. I tried to escape their grasp but the blanket was pulled too tight around me. They swung a leg over me like they were mounting a bucking horse. In my struggle, I managed to get the hand on my face to loosen allowing me to bite down into their pinkie. Small strands of hair found their way onto my tongue making me shiver. That hand came back down across my face, and it stung. Now it was around my throat. Thick fingers dug into my neck. I could not breathe. I got my own hands around his wrists, but I did not have any more strength to give to the fight.

My head grew light before he took his free hand and traced his fingers through my hair. He kissed my lips then finally pulled his hand from my neck. He backhanded me again across the other side of my face now.

I drew in ragged breaths and started coughing hard. Hard enough to shake my bed and hard enough that it caused my body to seize and bend with each sharp intake of breath. I was coughing so hard it caused me to heave. He was finally gone and I could move freely. I rolled over onto my side to relieve some of the pain from my stomach. When I finally caught my breath, my head caught up with me from its lack of oxygen, and I passed out from the pain and the exhaustion.

I went to shower the next morning and saw the condition that I was left in. My hair was even more of a mess than normal and my face and neck gave off a horrid unnatural color. Purple marks in the shapes of fingers wrapped around my neck and two red marks were still visible on my cheeks from where he slapped me. I knew who it was who left the marks. Bits of the hair from his hands were still trapped beneath my tongue. I was disgusted. Slowly peeling off my shirt revealed more marks on my chest from where he had groped me. He was so rough with them that they were sore to my touch.

I got in the shower with the water turned to its highest setting. With a firm grip, I dragged the rag roughly over my body until the skin turned red and raw. I did my best to wash away his touch but, no matter how rough I was with myself, I could still feel his grasp on me. I began to scrub my head to the point where I felt like I was pulling out my hair. Strands of blonde came away in my fingertips. It still was not enough. I grabbed a pair of scissors and began hacking away at my hair. My grip was shaky making the strands uneven, but I did not care. A slip of my hand caused me to miss my hair and cut through the top layer of the skin of my forearm. I dropped the scissors when the initial pain hit me, but I then felt a sudden wave of release. My head began to spin with curiosity as I glanced back down at the scissors now laying in the tub. I picked them up and held them open at the blade. With the grip tight in my right hand, I pressed them down into my left arm. Blood slowly trickled from the cut I had made and it hurt, but nothing hurt as much as what he did to me the night prior. With the desired pressure, I dragged the blade across my arm and felt the sweet sense of release it brought me. A sigh of relief escaped my lips.

*

Weeks went by and the more I stuck my head out of my room, the more he touched me. A morning reading on the couch in the living room led to an arm around my shoulders as a wandering hand reached for my chest. Meals at the dinner table turned into him rubbing my leg with his sweaty hands and playing footsie with me and running his feet up and down my legs. Mom's drinking got worse and brought about even more ignorance. I did not recognize the woman before me, or maybe I did? Their emptied beer bottles began piling up around the house and the home I once knew began to deteriorate before me. All of my time was spent in my room or at the library. Everywhere that I went, I made sure he could not follow. My door was locked to him and my mother and my scars became my best friends and the only ones I felt I could truly trust and rely on besides Sam, who never knew the horrors I faced. I felt dirty keeping those secrets from her, but with all of the things she had going on at home, what I was suffering through felt like a burden. All of the burdens made me feel even more guilty and filthy than he ever did.

Over and Over

I was late. God damnit I was late! It is my first day back to school, and I was already running late for my first class of the year. I ran into the main office and waited anxiously for the receptionist to write out my hall pass. She tore it away from its pad so slowly I felt like I was waiting years just in the fifteen seconds it took her. When she finally handed it to me, I snatched it from her and started running to my first class. *No running in the halls!* I slowed to a heavy-speed walk until I rounded the corner and was out of sight. Now I was at a dead sprint. *Room 116, room 116. Here it is.* I slowly turned the handle and pulled the door open. The teacher had just finished her roll call as I slipped inside and let the door close behind me. All she did was look at me and hold out a hand. Snickers came up around the room as I made my way up the center aisle to hand her my late slip.

"Most of the seats have already been claimed, but it looks like there's one over there next to Miss Marks." I turned to look where she was pointing and locked eyes with a girl that had a familiar head of black hair. I froze and it felt like my heart had leaped into my throat. "Any day now, Miss…?" My mind focused finally, and I remembered where I was.

"Cranston. Sarah Cranston." I walked over and slid onto the stool next to my new table partner. I almost over shot the seat and had to frantically catch myself on the table with how nervous I was. A few faces turned to look at me, and I could feel the heat rising in my cheeks. I put my head down and let my hair fall over my face.

"All right," the teacher began again, "I hope you have chosen your seats wisely because the person sitting next to you will be your lab partner for the rest of the school year." My head shot up. *What?*

I glanced over to my right and met the face of my lab partner through my hair. Her eyes were as bright a blue as when I first met her. The butterflies were back again and I still could not shake the feeling. I did not even know what the feeling was. She extended a hand to me and I froze.

"Nice to see you again." Her smile made my heart skip a beat.

"You too," I said, as I extended my own hand for her to shake.

"You do remember me, right?" A question that I was not prepared for. How could I forget her? She was the only one who was ever nice to me outside of Sam, even if it was only once. That and she saved me from that car a couple of years ago.

"Yeah," was all I could manage to get out. We finished shaking hands, but I could not find the will to let go. Her touch was so light and the skin on her hands was really soft. I could not stop staring into her eyes. So blue, so clear. She chuckled at me.

"You good?" She gestured toward her hand that I was still holding.

"Yeah. Sorry." I let go and pulled my own away, folding both together in front of me. I felt how clammy and sweaty they were. "I'm really sorry." I felt like I was turning an even deeper shade of red.

"It's okay," she chuckled while wiping her hand on her skirt. A short denim skirt with a black long-sleeve turtle neck that was so tight that it showed off her…

72

"Wow…"

"Wow, what?" I caught myself staring and shook myself back to her face.

"Nothing." She saw me staring and her face turned a bright red.

"Ladies, please, if I may return to my lecture now?"

"Sorry, Miss Harvey."

She turned back to the teacher and I did the same. With my notebook in front of me, I began taking notes for the day while stealing glances to my right at her. It went on all period until it finally ended with the bell and we went our separate ways at the door. People called her name out from the hall, *Andrea!* It was such a pretty name.

"Hey, Sarah!" I turned around to face her. "I'll see you tomorrow." All I did was nod and we finally went on to our next classes.

*

"I don't know, I just… I just can't describe it, you know?" I set the bar back on the hooks that held it in place and sat up on the bench. Weights and conditioning, the only way I could find another focus.

"I mean, have you ever felt this before?" Sam tapped my shoulder so I could move and let her have a go. She set her thirty-five-pound weights on the bar that I had to lift bare, something I would never see myself doing. One of the perks of being part of the varsity softball team, and the swim team, and the volleyball team. She would do the same thing on leg days nearly tripling my squat weight, yet, she looked thinner than most of the cheerleaders.

"The closest I have been was when I bumped into Danny in the hall. You know, the running back?"

"Oh, if I could have a piece of him..." she huffed. She always pushed herself too far but made it work. She finished her set and racked the weight. "Nice tits?"

"Sam!" My face went hot again, and I felt the corners of my lips curling. Sam turned to me.

"Does she?" I could not help but nod. "Right on. Not the main attraction though I'm assuming."

"Her eyes are super pretty," I said. Sam bit her bottom lip.

"Easy to get lost in?" She asked. I nodded again. "You, my dear, have a crush on her." I nearly dropped the weights that I had pulled off the bar.

"Wait, does that mean I'm...?" Sam shrugged at me.

"I could say so, but that's only if you act on it, I think. Hell, I had a crush on a girl once. Even had the nerve to kiss her." This is something new.

"Wait, what?"

"Yeah, then she punched me in the face and it started a brawl in the girls locker room." She set the weights back on the rack then took her position behind the bar again. "Of course, I won that fight." I lightly pushed against her stomach.

"You and your temper!" We both laughed.

"All right," she started, "push! You've got fifteen left in ya, I know it!"

*

Sam and I were sitting in the courtyard with our lunch trays at our lonely table on the edge of the collection. Of course, Sam was sitting *on* the table rather than on the bench like a normal human being. However, her legs made for a nice pillow on the days I was not feeling well. Thankfully, today was not one of those days. Not long after we finished eating, a newcomer came up to us. I could not see them.

"Hey there!"

"Well, hello there, stranger! What brings ya to these here parts?" Sam asked, a faux country accent in her tone.

"I thought, I would come over to her and say 'hello.'" Her voice, it sounded familiar.

"Well then, hello there. I'm Sam."

"Andrea." I heard their hands collide in a hand shake. So, it was her. "Wow, strong grip you've got there."

"Softball grip. You do any sports?"

"Cheerleading, but that's about it. Lame, I know."

"Figure like that, it makes sense." I heard Andrea cough.

"So, who's your friend?" *Fuck!* I slowly turned to face her.

"Hey, Andrea." I lifted a hand in a half assed wave.

"Oh hey! I didn't know you had this lunch period." I nodded. "Well then," she continued, "mind if I join you two then? All my other friends have the other lunch period."

"Well sure!" Sam chimed. "Go on ahead. There's a seat right there next to Sarah!" I gave her my *I hate you right now* look.

"I think I'll sit over here where I can see you guys." She set her bag down and the two of them began talking.

They talked for what felt like hours, even though there were only a few minutes in the lunch period. It was not like I was paying any attention. While they talked, I kept quiet and hid behind my hair again. However, I still got to see Andrea through the loose strands. She was perfect, and every time she laughed, every time she smiled, I got chills. Maybe Sam was right; maybe it was just a crush. I needed more time to think about it.

*

"Look, if you like her that much, then you *need* to tell her." Sam peeked her head above her locker while we changed out of our workout clothes.

"Or, hear me out, I don't tell her, we all stay friends, and I don't have to worry about her rejecting me." And then I can just sit here, a nervous wreck when we hang out together like we had been for the past month and a half.

"Look," Sam handed me a slip of paper over her locker. "I took the liberty of writing a letter from you to her on this little piece of paper."

"No…"

"Yes. You give it to her, and you don't have to do anything but give it to her." I took the note from her.

"How the fuck do you expect me to do that?"

"I don't know." Sam shrugged on her shirt. "Slip it in her locker, slip it in her bag or her lab book in class, or give it to her in person. All you have to do is make sure it gets to her." I thought about it for a moment while looking over the note. At least it was not written in what Sam called 'Sex Talk,' which she used more than I cared to admit.

I left the locker room and made my way to the hall where my school locker was. Andreas was just down the hall from mine, but I could never remember which one it was. I thought about how I wanted to give her the note on my way over, and the only way I could think to do it was to drop it through the slits in her locker's door. Cliché of me, but it got the job done, and I did not think I could muster up the courage to do it in person.

I collected my books from my locker and made my way to

76

the front of the school to go home. The block days were killing me, and so were the standardized tests. Not only were they testing us in every subject, but the block schedule also meant a new lunch schedule, which in turn meant I did not get to see Andrea as often as I wanted. It sucked, but it was just the way it needed to be for now. At least my anxiety had leveled out. I missed her though. I mean really missed her. Her smile, her laugh, her voice... oh god, if someone was in my head, they would think I had fallen in love with her, and maybe I had. I had never been in love before, and I was never really taught how to notice or recognize love. The way Sam describes it is *that feeling you get when you have a crush on someone but it's constant and you cannot shake the thought of them.* Made it sound like I was in love, to me.

Ugh... enough of this. I need to study.

*

October was here and the air was cold enough to force me into both a sweater and a hoodie. A disadvantage of being as small as I was; no body heat. At least it had not started snowing yet, but the clouds in the sky were beginning to tell me otherwise. Who I felt really bad for was the cheerleaders. Especially, because it was a Friday. Today was the final game of the playoffs and we were hosting our rival, which meant they were in their uniforms. Well, I guess I did not really feel bad for them as much as I felt bad for Andrea, but she actually had the 'body mass' to combat the cold as far as I thought. I blamed Sam for my train of thought.

I sat through the entire day without Andrea. She was not in class because of the pep rally and she spent lunch with the rest of the cheerleaders which meant the only time I would get to see her would be that night at the game, assuming I would be able to get out of the house. It was not like my mother would care anyway. She would probably be drunk and naked somewhere in the house with her boy toy by the time I got back.

Eventually, game time finally came around and Sam, and I found our spots near the top of the bleachers. It was perfect to give us a full view of the field. Personally, I was not a big football fan, but Sam absolutely loved it. She sat there telling me about the game and what was going on, but it all went in one ear and out the other. The only thing I kept my focus on was Andrea. She was showing off her moves in the squad. Though she was not the head cheerleader, she was definitely just as good. Even if I was a bit biased. It was in mentioning Andrea that I finally gave my full attention to Sam.

"Damn! She can hold her own down there, huh?" Sam was casually watching the performance, but I was completely mesmerized by it.

"She really can."

"That top isn't going to hold much though if she keeps throwing in all those flips." Sam nudged me.

"Seriously?" I could feel my cheeks getting hot enough to make them even more pink than the cold air already had.

"I'm kidding!" Sam started laughing. "Mostly…" she added.

I shook my head and tried to just enjoy the rest of the game. That was if I could have ever taken my eyes away from Andrea. It went by with ease and our team brought home an easy win. Everyone practically stormed the field; parents, girlfriends, even teachers. I stood back and waited with Sam for the crowd to die down a little before trying to approach the cheerleaders.

Sam nudged me with her elbow. "Are you gonna give it to

her?" With my hands in the pocket of my hoodie, I could feel the corners of the worn piece of paper.

"Yes… no… maybe… I don't know." I started to fidget with it.

"Well, you better think fast!" I looked up and there was Andrea jogging over to us.

"Hey, guys! Glad you could make it out." She hugged us both, and I could feel the warmth of her body on my own. She was so warm despite having on only a skirt and a long sleeve shirt. It made it that much more upsetting when she pulled away.

"We're glad we came!" Sam chimed. "You put on a hell of a show."

"Thanks! What did you think of the game, Sarah? I know it's not really your thing." I froze. I did not know what to say.

"I liked it," was all I managed to get out. *Bonehead response!* I spaced out again while Andrea and Sam talked. All I could think about was the damn note in my pocket while I stared mindlessly at Andrea.

"Well, the girls, and I are going out to celebrate. Do you guys wanna join us?" I looked over to the rest of the cheerleading squad and felt a chill colder than the weather run down my spine.

"I'm good," Sam replied. "But Sarah might be interested." Andrea looked at me.

"What do ya say?" I thought about it. There was no way I would be able to get a word with her if I went out with them. That and I did not want to deal with another late-night beating.

"I'll pass. I have a… uh… project that I need to work on for my English class." A white lie, but I was trying to work on extra credit to pull my grade up from the one test I missed.

"It's no problem. Hey, I'll see you two on Monday, yeah?"

"Definitely!" Sam chirped.

79

"Awesome! See you then!" and she was off, back to her world.

Sam turned to me. "What the hell was that?"

"I don't know." I pulled my hood over my eyes, embarrassed. "I panicked."

"You're giving it to her on Monday."

"Maybe."

"No, not 'maybe.' You *will* give it to her on Monday."

*

It was right before the first period and I was just standing there only fifteen feet away from her. The note was sitting in my hand collecting the sweat from my palm. I could not do it. What was I gonna say? How was I going to give it to her discreetly? So many thoughts in my head, my heart racing. I felt a light nudge in my back. It was Sam.

"Now's your chance," she said. I went to move, but hesitated. Sam nudged me again.

"Okay," I said, taking a deep breath, and I made my way over to her.

Broken

I awoke to the grey light of dawn as it shined through the cracked panes of my window. My nostrils twitched as they picked up the all too familiar smell of cigarette smoke and old booze. I could not help, but cringe at the sound of my mother's headboard slamming against the wall as it echoed through the thin walls of our house. My blood began to run cold and it sent shivers down my spine at the mere image of him... No, I was not going to go there that morning.

Sluggishly, I began to crawl from my mattress on the floor. The old heap left my body stiff and caused my muscles to ache and my joints to pop as I stretched out my limbs. My blonde hair draped over my eyes, and I had to practically fish through the knotted mess to be able to see properly. Luckily, it was the only adjustment I had to make for myself. Being one of the girls at school who was less endowed had its benefits, though it did spark some major teasing in the locker room.

My legs turned to jelly as I stood, and I had to throw out my arms just to keep from falling ass first back onto the concrete like slab on the floor. I eventually got myself moving and began the trek to the guest bathroom. Ironic given we never actually had anyone over. I stepped cautiously over a hole in the floor that was caused by my own fat foot just the other day. We either needed a carpenter or pest control, or possibly both. It did make me think of the gash in my calf, and I looked down to observe the cut. Staring back at me was a deep red scar outlined by a gorgeous purple bruise. Lovely.

The banging in the walls finally stopped when I reached the bathroom, and it was coincidentally replaced by a series of shouting. What else was new? I ignored it and peeled back the loose shirt from my body. As if by habit, I began to observe myself judgingly in the mirror. Ordinary face that nobody ever found attractive, that was still a thing. Small mounds on my chest that was the foundation for their jokes, yep, still small. Rounded cigarette burns on my neck, bruises from being choked out by my stepfather, fresh cut in my forehead from having a beer bottle thrown at me the night prior, scars that lined my arms, yep, everything was still there.

I stole my eyes away from the mirror and turned on the tub's faucet, setting the knob to the highest temperature setting. It was not long before steam began to fill the room, and I stepped inside the tub. Scalding water washed over my body and burned away at my skin. I shuddered through deep breaths while I adjusted to the heat. Pain was my friend; pain was my ally. I cleansed myself through gritted teeth as I fought back the screams I had become so used to suppressing.

I shut off the water and stepped out into the steam filled room. Fog had densely covered the mirror, clouding my reflection as small beads raced toward the countertop. I picked up one of the razor blades from the cracked surface and began tracing it along the deep scars on my arm, but I did so softly, trying not to let it penetrate the skin. I did it simply to remind me of its presence as the cold steel tickled and glided up the soft underside of my arm. It tempted me to dig deeper into the warm, dampened flesh. I set it back in its place. Maybe later, I needed to get ready for the day's classes.

I dressed myself in the clothing colored to represent what I pictured to be the color of my soul, black. Black hoodie, black jeans, black sneakers, everything was black. If only I could afford black hair dye. I pulled the hood over my head in an attempt to hide myself. Unsatisfied, I pulled some loose golden strands over my eyes, enough to hide them, but little enough as to not obscure my vision.

The hardest part was trying to leave. It was always a chore seeing as though my parents had always managed to migrate to the living room in their half drunken state. My bag sat lazily by the front door, but my headphones I found lying on the kitchen table where I was last working on homework, now drenched in beer. Those would never work again. Thanks, *dad.* I grabbed my bag by the door and was set to leave before a voice interrupted me.

"Hey!" It was deep and disgruntled. A book slammed against the back of my head. "Don't leave your shit lying around." I picked it up and saw it was the novel I was reading for AP Lit, also soaked in beer.

"Yes, sir," I responded weakly. I was not in the mood to deal with his shit that day.

"Look at me when you're talking to me!" he barked. I did not want to turn and look, but refusing an order meant more abuse. As if I was not going to get it anyway. I turned and looked him in the eyes, bloodshot. My eyes glanced downward, and I instantly regretted it. Just below the hem of his shirt hung what could only be meekly described as a limp noodle. A short, pink, misshapen noodle. I tried not to vomit at the sight. "Be home by five."

"Yes, sir," and I turned to leave.

"I'm not done talking to you!" but I was already slipping out the door. I slammed it behind me as the crash of another thrown beer bottle sounded from the other side. No doubt aimed at where I had been previously standing.

Finally, the outside world. It was still dark and full of assholes like my stepdad, but I did not think anyone could be nearly as bad as he was. I pulled out my phone to check my text messages. I tried talking to Andrea, but she never responded, and apparently still had not. I feared the worst. We had been best friends since she moved here and she never left my side. A pain began to form in my thoughts. As if it was not already hard enough to make friends, coming out as a bisexual with romantic feelings for your best friend of the same sex made it even harder.

*

I held the note in clammy hands. Sweat formed on my brow as I approached her locker. Raven black hair draped over her perfect head, a face so perfect it gave diamonds a run for their money, a figure that made over half the girls at school jealous, and those gorgeous sapphire blue eyes that sparkled under the fluorescent lights. That was Andrea, who was my best friend and my biggest crush since she moved to this school. It was the day I would finally tell her. I approached her sheepishly. My legs felt like they were being weighed down by concrete blocks.

"Hey, Sarah! Are you feeling okay?" She looked me up and down, a concerned expression on her face. I could feel the heat rise in my face.

"H-hey, Andrea." I brushed a strand of hair behind my ear. "I'm fine. I have something for you." I looked down at the note I held in my hands.

"Is it another one of those boys from the basketball team? I told them I'm not interested." She graciously took the note from

84

my shaking hands and swiftly opened it. I watched as her eyes scanned the college-ruled paper, her facial expression never changing all the way to the end. She scoffed. "Yeah, just another love note." She moved to put it away in her pocket before she did a double take. My heart had jumped into my throat. She looked the note over again and then looked at me. Back at the note. Back at me. I could not take the suspense, and I felt like running away. She folded the note back up and placed it delicately back in my hands before it was snatched from her by the head cheerleader. Oh no.

"What's this, Andrea? Another admirer?" She flipped it back open and read it herself. Double oh no. "Oh... my... god."

"Sydney don't." but Andrea was cut off.

"This is rich." Just when things couldn't get worse, more cheerleaders began surrounding us. They all read it, and they all laughed. I was so embarrassed I felt like I was shrinking.

I looked up to Andrea, but her expression had become a dark mix of anger and embarrassment. She snatched the letter and stormed off, making sure to toss it in the dumpster as she went.

"Andrea!" I called, but she kept walking.

The girls began laughing at me and mocking me. I couldn't help but sink against the lockers behind me as they crowded even closer. Their chants grew louder. My emotions darkened.

"All right, break it up!" After a couple minutes, Sam's voice came up over everyone. The girls left but I didn't have the energy to stand. She lent a hand to me and I graciously took it. "Are you okay, Sarah?"

"Y-yeah. I'm fine," I said in between sniffles.

"Hey, don't worry about them. They don't know what they're talking about." She looked at me with pity and sorrow in her face. "Hey, you know I love you and you'll always have me.

You know that, right? You're my best friend." She pulled her half of our necklace from her shirt and presented it to me. I just stared at it and wanted to pull out my half, but I could not find the strength.

"Thanks," I said with a weak smile. "But I just need to be alone right now." I turned and stormed off, leaving Sam standing in the hall, alone. It was the first time I had abandoned her, but nothing struck more than the abandonment I was feeling from Andrea.

*

A loud horn sounded from my left as a metro bus roared past me, barely missing my right foot that was extended out into the street. I stumbled and fell backwards, spilling my bag's contents into the gravel behind me. As I tried to collect my things, I noticed that my face was wet, and I was short of breath. Had I been crying? It came subtly at first, but I could feel the lump forming in my throat. Before I knew it, I was sobbing into my knees while I heaved out ragged gasps. I was crying uncontrollably at that point, and I could not stop it. Flashes of having the blade in my hand from earlier that morning came back to me, and I blamed myself for not sending it deeper into my skin. Who knew that one incident from six months earlier would ruin everything?

I wiped my eyes and kept walking. It was a dazed walk as I suppressed all my thoughts that were not related to walking to school and breathing, counting my steps as I went to aimlessly fill my mind. Before I knew it, I had reached the school. Checking my phone told me two things; that I was still an hour early, and that I still had no reply from Andrea. As if she was going to. It was the first time I had tried to talk to her since that day and it Probably did not help that I actively avoided her after that and did not see much of her on campus in the days that followed me telling her.

With the time to spare, I decided to make my way toward the school library. It was my safe space. The cheerleaders never came in to bother me, it was quiet, and I could work in peace enveloping myself in my books. I opened the door and froze in my tracks. Of all days, on my worst one yet, I was met by an all too familiar sight. Raven black hair.

She faced me; I grew stiff as a board. She smiled sheepishly; I began to sweat. Every muscle and fiber in my body told me one thing, run. I did. I ran as the emotions came flooding back to me.

"Wait! Sarah!" she called. I did not turn back. I ran until I was locked in the girl's bathroom upstairs. Tears streamed down my face and sweat leaked from every pore of my body. I could not do it. Angered by my growing weakness, I punched out part of the bathroom mirror. Glass shards littered all over the floor.

A knock came at the door. "Sarah, please! I need to talk to you!" I ignored her.

I slouched down into the far corner near the sinks and cried. I could feel my eyes growing puffy and my nose running as it came uncontrollably. The glass shards shined on the bathroom floor and one managed to find its way into my hand. More knocks came from the door as I rolled up my sleeve. The banging was relentless, but so were my tears. I touched the glass to my wrist and pressed it down. Blood seeped from my skin uncontrollably and dripped onto the floor. I bit back the pain and pressed further. The blood oozed faster, telling me I was almost there. I raked the shard across my wrist leaving a never-ending gushing wound. The shard swapped hands, and I followed suit on the other wrist.

Everything began to fade. The banging grew more and more muffled as I slipped into a daze. Everything was cold. Darkness swept over my eyes as I began to slip. The last thing I heard was the muffled sound of the door slamming against the wall and someone shouting my name.

"Sarah! Sarah! God damnit!"

My vision clouded as the world around me was shrouded by darkness.

*

It was slow. Why was everything so blurry? My head, it... it hurt. Why was it so dark? Where was I? Rhythmic beeping, sharp pain in my arms, no, my hands? It was in my wrists. I could hear a pump. What kind though? Everything seemed to echo. I wanted to move but my body hurt. Everything hurt, but everything was all so numb. How did I get there? I finally managed to drop my head to the right. There is someone there, asleep in the chair by the window. Someone else was there. They were dressed in all blue, a light blue.

"Hey there," they said. It was a female. "How are you feeling?" she asked. I tried to talk, but my mouth felt dry and my lips would not move. "It's okay. Dehydration is common. Just rest. I'll be right back with some water." She left me alone in the room.

Everything was still spinning and I made efforts to focus on something to bring my mind back into focus. My eyes wandered until they fell on the stranger sitting in the chair. The blurs came in waves and it split my head even more. Squinting, I felt like I was able to make out some of their features. Long hair, black. I could see their chest rise and fall, and I could see the shape of their breasts, so it has to be another female, but who. I tried squinting to work out more of their face, but my head was pounding. I gave up as the girl in blue came back with my water.

"Here you go, sweetie. Now, don't drink it too fast. You might make yourself sick." I nodded lightly. "Do you need anything else?" I shook my head. "Okay, hit the button if you need anything." Again, I nodded, then let my face fall back on the girl in the chair. Who was she and why was she there? I was too tired and eventually fell back asleep.

When I woke up again, the room had changed. Light now shined in through the window, but the shades were closed to keep the room on the darker side. There were some new noises in the room, one sounded like static, the other sounded like someone talking, but I could not make out who. Maybe it was another nurse? No, the static and the voices went hand in hand. I turned my head to where the girl was when I went back to sleep, but the chair sat empty. So much for my company. Then again, I spent most of my time alone anyway. I thought about it for a moment. The sounds, the static, the voices. It had to be a TV or radio so, who was changing the station? I did my best to sit up, but my wrists still hurt so I had to scoot up on my elbows. A small grunt escaping my throat.

"Oh my God, Sarah! Thank goodness you're awake!" Someone came rushing over so fast, they startled me. I was quickly wrapped in a hug as black hair smothered my face. It smelt like lavender. Black hair, lavender shampoo. Only one person I know fit that description.

"Andrea?" I asked in a hoarse whisper.

"Well, no shit, Sherlock. My God, I'm so glad you're okay." I felt her arms tighten around me.

"What… what happened? Where are we?" Andrea pulled

back and I could finally see her face. Her expression looked like a mix of worry and sadness with a hint of scorn and anger.

"You don't remember?" I shook my head, embarrassed. She sighed. "Sarah, you're in the hospital." Finally, I slowly looked around. The white tiled ceiling, the white canvased bedsheets, the beeping of my heart monitor, a small TV mounted on the wall, tubes and cords that traveled to my arm; my arms. Both of them, from my wrists and halfway up my forearms, were wrapped in bandages. It was a lie; I did remember. I remembered someone calling for me, the ambulance ride over, paramedics struggling to stabilize me, and, at one point, the long drawn out resonation of a flatline.

"I... I almost..." I could not find the words to describe how I was feeling.

"I know." I looked at her and there were the beginnings of tears in her eyes.

"I'm so sorry," I whispered. Tears began to well up in my own eyes, but mine overflowed. I felt their warmth slide down my cheeks. I looked at her and her eyes were full of rage.

"What the fuck were you thinking?" I thought about the events leading up to it and tried to find the words to express myself.

"I... it was too much." The pain inside welled up again. I wanted my release and instinctively grabbed my wrist. It shot up my arm and I felt it. I could feel the pain again. and I could not tell if it was emotional or physical. I broke down. Andrea wrapped me up in another hug, but more tender and loving this time. I wanted to embrace her myself, but I was too weak and resolved to bury my face into her shoulder. The tears just kept flowing out. Her shirt was probably getting stained, but she never pulled away. She just let me cry it out right there in her arms, and

90

I was thankful for it, but also confused.

I finally got a hold of myself and managed to stop the tears and pull away from her, but she made sure to keep a hand on mine. There were so many questions I wanted to ask her, but there was only one I felt like I *needed* to ask her.

"Why did you come back?" I wiped the tears from my eyes and sniffed back the snot dripping from my nose.

"Because you're my best friend. Why else?"

"What about the note?"

"What note?" I looked at her and met her eyes before looking back down at my lap in shame. "Oh, that note…" she said, recognition in her voice. "I… uh… well…"

"I knew it. I wasted my time with it all." I felt defeated.

"No, you didn't." I looked back up at her. "Listen," she began again, "I have been confused about a lot of things for a while now and that was one of them. I just didn't know how to go about them."

"I was a coward for not coming to you sooner or even telling you with my own words for that matter."

"No, Sarah. I was the coward. You had the courage to actually tell me. And, to be honest…" I could feel my heart pounding in my throat. "Look, I really like you, Sarah, more than I can even put into words. This is all just weird to me, and so new."

"Yeah, me too." We both looked away from one another.

"But…"

"But?"

"I am willing to learn with you, about all of this."

"Really?" I felt like I was a bit more excited than I should have been,

"Really." I could not help but smile.

She pulled me into another hug and I did my best to do the same. The pain shot through my wrists and up my arms, but I forced them both around her neck. It hurt so bad but now, I at least had a good reason to be in pain.

Enemies

I had my books tucked tightly under my arms that I had folded tightly over my chest. Daunting stares drifted in my direction from the other students and it was a task to not dart my eyes back and forth across the hall at them. I could not sink further under my hood even if I tried. My gaze swept to the right and the students were replaced by a tight black fabric. I looked up to catch sight of Andrea's all too familiar black turtleneck sweater as she looped an arm through the little bit of space I had in mine. It was hard not to lean into her as she drew me in. She was calming, and the tighter I found myself pressed against her, the calmer I found myself.

"Sup, love birds!" Sam's wedge of a face dove in between us as she threw an arm over each of our shoulders. "What the fuck are *you* staring at?" she snarled at a group of onlookers. A pebble compared to the number of people who were, but I had to chuckle at the idea of their panicked faces as they hurried away from our little ensemble.

"Someone is chipper this morning?" Andrea said, the question implied in her tone.

"Well..." she began. "I may have just caught the attention of Brad Newman."

I felt the shock on my face. "The quarterback?"

"Who knew he was into fit bitches?" Sam quipped.

"That, or, he is just a huge fan of how goofy you can be?"

"Andrea! I am hurt!" Her arms disappeared from our

shoulders. "And here, all this time, I thought we were friends!" We looked back, and she had an arm over her face and the other flung out behind her.

"You are ridiculous." I scoffed

"Well, it was worth a shot," she said, still holding her pose. The bell rang for the first period and everyone in the hall started scurrying toward the doors that lined the halls. "First period English which means…" Sam sided up against me again and took me by the arm. "This little specimen is now mine until third period biology." It was weird feeling the competitive tug between the two but Andrea loosened her grip, and I almost longed for it.

"Very well," she said. Then to me, "I'll see you later." She gave my hand a squeeze and leaned down to kiss my cheek. I felt the heat rise in my own as she started to pull away.

I grabbed her hand harder, "Wait!" and I pulled her down to me enough so my lips could brush against hers. So soft and warm. They tasted like strawberries. "Love you," I said sheepishly.

"Love you too," she said, putting a finger to my nose.

"All right, get a room!" Sam griped and she pulled me away. "We're gonna be late."

I looked back at Andrea and she looked toward me with a smirk and a wave. She was damn pretty, and I could not help but want to stare while Sam dragged me along. I kept trying to look back while Sam dragged me around the corner and down toward the English hall. People kept staring at us as we walked, but quickly turned away once they saw the look on Sam's face. It made for a quick walk with most people parting out of our way in the otherwise crowded hallway.

Shields's class was one of the few classes that grabbed my attention anymore. I pulled out the leather bound Shakespeare collection I kept in my bag for the class and turned to where we had left off in *Hamlet*. Even though we were past the part of reading the play; I still preferred to read it along with the film adaptation he had playing from the projector. It made it easier to find the changes and the lines that were omitted from the script. It was one of my favorite plays, and I found it hard to see it taken for granted sometimes. Like they said, "The book is always better."

A light snoring echoed in my ear, and I glanced from the page to see Sam with her head laid over the back of her chair, sound asleep. Of course, no one noticed, with us sitting in the back of the classroom. Even Shields was oblivious with his face buried in his laptop either watching the play or grading our essays. I took out one of my pencils and poked her in the face and received no reaction from her. As I went to put the pencil back in its case, it felt wet on one end and I had to glance back at Sam. Down the side of her face was the biggest string of drool sliding down the side of her cheek and dripping off her chin. It amazed me she only needed me going over her essays in order for her to keep a passing grade in the class. A better reader than a writer, and her math skills were atrocious. The bell rang to end class and she nearly fell out of her seat. I had to hide a chuckle behind my hand.

The two of us got through gym class the same as we always did. Sam did a lot of heavy lifting and it took us taking off all the weight she lifted for me to even get the bar off the rack. Though, she was impressed to say that I had improved. So was our teacher when I was able to lift more than my body weight when it came to my max out tests. Of course, Sam still held the girls' record for the school, and even had half the boys in the class beat. It was the only class she did not ask for help in. Of course, everything outside of gym and English was remedial classes for her as well as a study hall to fill the extra elective slot she had. Her next was remedial algebra while I went off to my advanced biology class, the only class that I shared with Andrea.

By the time I walked through the door, Andrea was already waiting at our lab counter for me and gave a very high-stretched wave from across the room. A seat by the windows where we could look out at the rose bushes grown by the agriculture class. Sometimes, they let us play with their genetics, and I could see the purple and red petals of the strain Andrea, and I had messed with. Our teacher did not know how we had managed to get them to grow like that and said they were as remarkable as they were improbable. I just thought they were pretty, and I could not help but take a glance out the window to see how much they had grown in. Andrea had to prop her head up on my shoulder to get my attention.

"Whatcha starin at?" Her voice vibrated in my ear and sent a chill down my side and made me shiver.

"I am looking at the roses," I said leaning slightly into her. She gave just enough push back to make it feel like I was leaning against her. It felt like she had a hand around my side, and I loved that supportive feeling.

"Well, aren't you two cute?" The snarky voice echoed behind us, and I could not help, but to turn red and try to lift myself up off Andrea, but she held firm and it felt like she was pulling me in even more.

"What do you want, Barnes?" she asked. I forgot that Rebecca was in the class with us. She was one of the three fliers for the cheer squad. At least that is what I was told.

"Oh, nothing. I just wanted to see how our two *lovebirds* were doing." I could not see her, but I could feel the air quotes around the word 'lovebirds.'

96

"Save it," Andrea barked. "We both know you don't give two shits about our relationship."

"You're right, I don't. But you know wha…"

"Go away, Rebecca."

"Or what? Are you gonna sick your dyke on me?"

"No, but you may not make it down from your next flight without an injury."

"Is that a threat?"

"It might be…" Andrea growled.

"Ms. Barnes, can you please take your seat so that we may get started?" The boom from Misses Caldwell echoed through the room as did the chuckles from the rest of the class.

I took my head off Andrea's shoulder and watched a red-faced Rebecca skulk away with her head down to the back of the classroom. When I looked back to the front, Misses Caldwell was looking our way and gave us a wink. I mouthed her a *thank you,* and she nodded in return before beginning her lesson on mitochondria. The entire time, Andrea and I had our stools almost on top of one another with our ankles crossed to the other's stool. It felt like no time at all before the bell was ringing and we had to part ways until the end of the day.

"So," Andrea began. "I'll see you tonight after I get out of practice, right?" I nodded, still too starstruck and lost in her eyes to say anything. "Good." She leaned down and gave me a kiss on the cheek and a touch on the tip of my nose with her finger. "See you," she said and she walked away.

"See you," I mumbled, but she was already half way down the hall.

*

The library was always quiet, and the librarian never cared that I spent all of my time there after school. She even tried to help me occasionally with my history homework, finding books and sources for me to use in my essays and research papers. I sat at one of the computer terminals looking at articles and history sites about Germany's Third Reich as well as had three bookmarked pages in books about both the rise and fall of the Nazi party. A ten-page research paper was due by the end of the semester and worth the same amount as our final grade. I needed it to be perfect. It *was* going to be perfect. Especially with the hours I put in day after day waiting for Andrea to get out of cheer practice.

I felt a pair of arms wrap around my neck from behind and my nose was filled with the smell of lavender. The hand I had laid in front of the keyboard came up to cup over where Andreas crossed. She rested her chin on the top of my head.

"Whatcha working on?"

I could not help but chuckle. "I'm working on my research paper for history."

"The semester project?" I nodded. "Don't we still have a month before that's due?"

"We do, but with all this time that I have had in the library waiting for you, I've managed to have it close to finished."

"Really?" She took her head off my shoulder and looked at me sideways with her hands on my shoulders. "How much do you have left?"

"About a page and a half give or take." I shrugged.

"Can you help me with mine since you'll have so much free time?"

"If you're asking me to write your paper, you know I can't." I looked and saw she was giving me a pouty lip and added a little quiver for good measure. I sighed then gave her a smile. "If I know your topic, I'll help you find your sources, but that's it." She gave me a big hug.

"Thank you, love! Now, are you ready to get out of here?"

"If you let me close down the computer, yes."

She let me go and we walked to her car. It was already dark out, and there were only a few other cars in the parking lot. A few of the cheerleaders were still hanging around outside and staring in our direction. It was a little bit of a walk from the library to where she parked, and we had to go through the hoard, which included the triage of fliers. Rebecca walked up with both Julia and Ashley in tow and partially blocked our way to Andrea's car.

"Really?" Andrea asked them. Her arm dropped from my shoulder and she stepped slightly in front of me as if to protect me.

"Science bitch isn't here to save you this time, is she?"

"Back off of us, Barnes!"

"Or what?" Julia asked. "Your dyke hound isn't here to help you either."

"You leave Sam out of this!" My hand went half the way to my mouth and my jaw clenched. All three cheerleaders looked at me, one of them disgusted, Rebecca.

"You have something to say?" she asked angrily. I stood there staring. "Hey! I'm talking to you! Do you have something to say to me?" She took a step toward me. I shook my head. "That's what I fucking thought. Little bitch!" She pushed me at my chest and I stumbled backwards and into the asphalt.

I heard skin hit skin, and then an ear splitting scream rang out around the parking lot. Turning my head, I saw Rebecca curled up on the ground clutching at the side of her face and crying. Julia and Ashley were on either side of her trying to calm her down. Ashley looked up at Andrea who was partially looming over them while also standing to where I had to look between her knees to see what was going on. It was the first time Ashley spoke up during the whole thing.

"Crazy ass bitch! What the fuck is wrong with you?" Andrea did not say anything and kept staring at them.

I could not see her face and did not know the look she was giving them, but after a few seconds, Ashley's face grew with fear as well as Julia's. They helped a still sniveling Rebecca to her feet and rushed away from us. Andrea turned around and took a moment to collect herself. Her eyes were closed and her lips formed a thin line. She took a deep breath before looking down at me with a loving smile and held a hand out to help me to my feet. I smiled back, ignoring the cold wetness forming on my arm.

"Come on," she said, tilting her head toward her car. "Let's get you home."

*

We sat out in front of my house for a few moments staring at the front door. There was one light on in the front room and none lit upstairs. They were still eating or fucking on the sofa again, something I came to ignore along with the beer and liquor bottles strewn about with the musty stench my childhood home had accumulated over the last seven years. I hated walking in the door anymore and hated climbing the stairs to my room with my mattress laid out on the floor.

Andrea placed a hand on my knee, and I looked away from the window. She had the softest smile on her face, and I could not help but smile back at her. Her hand went from my knee to my cheek and we sat there staring at one another in the dark of her car with her thumb running back and forth. I brought my hand up to hers and felt like melting into her and closed my eyes. She started to hum a tune I did not recognize, but it was beautiful regardless. I leaned over her center console and rested my head on her pillow of a chest, and she wrapped her arms around me and pulled me in tight. I did not want to leave.

"Don't worry; you'll see me in the morning," she said soothingly as if reading my mind.

"You say that every night," I chuckled. The lump was already forming in my throat, and I could feel the tears trying to escape my eyes.

"I do, but it comes true every day, doesn't it?" I nodded. "Good, so long as you know." She put a finger under my chin and gently lifted my head off her chest. "I love you," she whispered.

"I love you too." I fought with everything I had to keep my voice from trembling.

As if pulling my chin with her thumb and index finger, she brought me in for a kiss. It lasted for what felt like minutes, but at the same time felt like milliseconds when our lips parted.

"I'll see you in the morning," she said. I nodded and gave her one more quick peck on the lips before opening her car door and trudging my way through dead grass up to my front door.

Going from outside to inside, I felt no change in temperature making the only striking difference the change in lighting. Even then, the room was still dark. A single dim lamp was lit in the corner near the window while a faint glow from the TV lit a small portion of the room in front of the stained couch. I eased the door shut and made my way toward the stairs. My foot barely hit the first step when I heard the ritual snap coming from the couch and froze.

101

"Come here," my stepfather's voice echoed in the near empty room. I obeyed and walked over to stand in front of him. Three cigarette scars told me not to do otherwise. He patted the couch next to him with that creepy smile he always wore when first addressing me. "Sit down," he cooed.

"No, sir." I stood there in front of him and put my head down, my hands gripping the strap on my bag.

"Fine, bad cop it is," he grumbled. He was annoyed. "Do you have any idea what time it is?" I shook my head. "Seven thirty, school gets out at three. So, where were you?"

"Library."

"Why?"

"Working on a school project."

"You can't do that here?"

"We don't have a computer here."

"Well," he began again. "Be that as it may," he burped, then sat up and reached for the beer bottle on the coffee table in front of him. His robe came open slightly, and I saw the tuft of chest hair he liked to flaunt about from my top peripherals. "Your mother was worried sick about you."

"I'm sorry." Bull shit, I knew she was not worried. "Where is Mom?"

"Sleeping." This time he stood up and walked around the table toward me. "So, it looks like it's just you and me tonight." He chuckled, and I could smell the alcohol on his breath.

"I already ate," I grumbled even though all I had was a protein bar that I got from Miss Levey. I shoved past him and toward the stairs. The bottle he was holding smashed against the floor behind me from his drunken short throw. Warm, stale beer splashed against my calves, but I kept walking and made my way upstairs.

102

"Fine! Be that way!" he shouted after me. "Fucking whore bag bitch!"

I slammed the door to my room and dropped my bag at the foot of my mattress. I did not even bother to change or turn on the light. Flinging myself against the old springs and burying my face in my pillow, the tears I held back with Andrea finally began to seep through as I silently wept to sleep and became bombarded with nightmares that never went away.

*

I walked the half a mile to school with the sun barely shining through the cloud filled horizon. The air was no different than any other cold morning. It never went below the forties on even some of the coldest days of the year, and the only reason it was ever that cold was because of the clouds. Walking in the front door did show something different for the first time. There were two adults I did not recognize as teachers standing around in the lobby talking loudly with our principal who had a pained look once she made eye contact with me. She gestured me toward her with her finger then pointed toward the counsel room. I nodded and went in.

There were four other girls in the room. Andrea sat off to the left of the table by herself with Julia, Ashley, and Rebecca sitting across from her. I walked over and sat down beside Andrea and was about to ask her what was going on before she shook her head at me. The look on her face was frustration and she had her arms crossed over her chest. I looked across the table at the other three, two of which were holding a very similar stance, except for Rebecca whose smile was quirked in a sinister smirk almost pointing toward the dark purple bruise on her cheek. Andrea must have gotten her good in the parking lot. It looked like it still hurt the way she kept trying to poke at it.

We sat there for a while before more people came in to join us. Our principal sat at the head of the table with the cheer coach and basketball coach behind her. Next came the two adults I did not know who stood behind the three fliers in front of us. Finally, the school's police officer walked in and practically shoved Sam into the room and down into the seat next to me making a sandwich out of the three of us. She kept squirming and trying to make herself comfortable in her seat. When I finally looked over, I saw her hands were caught behind her back, handcuffed.

"Would you like to tell us what happened, Miss Jones?" the basketball coach started.

"I keep telling you," Sam groaned. "I have no idea why you have me in here."

"Really?" she continued. "You have no idea what happened with a black eye staring you in the face like that?"

"No, I don't."

"Miss Barnes?" the cheer coach asked.

"That dyke wasn't there," Rebecca piped.

"Call me 'dyke' one more time and I'll wish I *did* give you that damn shiner!"

"Enough!" our principal shouted. "Then who did that to you?" I looked up to see Rebecca staring at Andrea. My eyes shifted between her and our principal. "Really?" she asked. "I would never have suspected one of our top students." She seemed exasperated and then looked at Andrea. "Why?"

"She came after Sarah," she said after a few seconds.

"Lying bitch! I never touched your little whore girlfriend!"

"That's enough, Rebecca," her mother chimed. My own would have slapped me across the face.

104

"Can you prove this?" our principal asked.

"Yes, I can." Andrea looked at me. "I saw the scrape on her arm after Rebecca pushed her over."

I was confused; I did not remember being injured from the fall. Andrea gestured to my hoodie, and I started to take it off. I set it on the table and rolled up my sleeves. On one arm, I felt the bumps in my arm and held it up for myself and the rest of the room to see. There were still bits of little black rocks lodged in it along with the light road rash around them. After letting them look, I pulled my sleeves back down over my arms and my hands trying to hide as much skin as possible. As much as I wanted to help Andrea out of this mess, I also did not want her to see the fresh cuts that matched the rest along my forearms.

"Bitch probably did that herself!" Rebecca barked. "We've all seen the razor blade cuts on her arms!"

"That's enough, Rebecca." Our principal looked at me and opened her mouth to speak when mine and Andrea's biology teacher walked into the room.

"Sorry I'm late," Miss Caldwell sang. "What did I miss?"

"Your students here," our principal began gesturing to the three of us in question. "They were telling us about our little encounter they had last night that have led to some serious assault claims."

"Miss Jones is not one of my students."

"She's not involved apparently." Our principal let out a heavy sigh.

"Then why is she still in cuffs?" Miss Caldwell asked, her gaze directed at the police officer. He looked at our principal and she nodded.

"Miss Jones," our principal began. "You along with Miss Shay and Miss Carson can return to class." The two of them got up with a huff and were first out the door.

"Good luck," Sam said. She shot me and Andrea a reassuring glance before closing the door behind her.

"Miss Caldwell, your professional opinion?" Our principal stared at her intently.

"What's the story?" she asked.

"The story is that Miss Marks assaulted Miss Barnes after an altercation involving Miss Barnes and Miss Cranston."

Miss Caldwell looked at me and Andrea with a questioning gaze. I looked back at her and lifted my sleeve again to show the scrapes on my arm and she nodded at me to put them down. She then looked at Rebecca and observed the bruise on her cheek for a moment before looking back at our principal. The police officer took a step toward Andrea with his cuffs still in hand, but Miss Caldwell stopped him with a raise of her hand.

"Those won't be necessary," she said. He stepped back against the wall and stood there waiting. "This may be new information to those here that weren't involved." She gestured toward Rebecca. "I have witnessed Miss Barnes's threats and homophobic slurs first hand…"

"As have we all," the principal interrupted, annoyed.

"… in my own classroom, especially yesterday in an attempt to disrupt my lesson." Miss Caldwell glared at our principal whose eyes shifted from her to Rebecca.

"Is this true, Miss Barnes?" she asked. Rebecca shrugged. "Coach, your suggestion?" The cheer coach looked at both Rebecca and Andrea.

"Violence is not tolerated on our team. As of now, the two of you are suspended and benched from the cheer team. You will be allowed to participate in practice mainly to train two replacements for us." She sighed. "Unfortunately, that means

106

hosting a second tryout for some of the girls that did not make it the first time and wasting time for that as well. Do you two understand the situation you have put me in?"

"Yes, ma'am," Andrea chimed without hesitation.

"Miss Barnes?"

"Yeah, whatever," she scoffed.

"You three are dismissed." We got up to leave, and I shuffled awkwardly out the door in front of Andrea.

"Fucking bitch," Rebecca mumbled as she parted in the other direction.

Andrea scoffed and grabbed my hand, pulling me away from the main office and back toward the English hall. Sam was waiting for us just around the corner and ambushed us as we came around, wrapping an arm around each of us. It was an awkward hug with Sam at nearly a forty-five-degree angle and my face half-buried in her chest. She sat there squeezing us for a moment before letting us go.

"Are you guys, okay?"

"Yeah, we're fine," Andrea grumbled.

"What happened?"

"Cheer suspension, I don't know for how long."

"But you're one of their best girls!" Sam whined

"Not good enough apparently," she said, shaking her head.

I reached out and gave her hand a squeeze. She squeezed back but quickly pulled her hand free and left us alone in the middle of the hall.

"I'll see you guys later!" she called back. We stared at the back of her black tuft of hair as she disappeared down the hall.

"What was that about?"

"I don't know," I sighed.

Sam put an arm around my shoulder and led me down

107

toward Shields's classroom, the entire time I was thinking about Andrea. I barely watched the *Hamlet* movie and barely tried to lift any of the weights in gym class. By the time biology came around, I was almost sprinting through the halls so that I could see her, but her seat was empty when I arrived. Rebecca glared at me as I took my seat by the window, and I could feel her eyes on me almost every second of the class. I did not take any notes and I should have for her. Andrea never showed up to class and I never saw her in the library that day. I walked home alone hoping and wishing she was okay.

My Immortal

You know that feeling, when someone really likes someone else, and they cannot for the life of them get rid of the butterflies in their stomach? That was me. Every time I met up with Andrea, my heart did flips in my stomach, and it takes up until we go our separate ways to finally get it to settle back into my chest where it belongs. Not that it mattered. It would start doing flips again the next time I saw her anyway. I just could not help it that she was so beautiful.

I went through my next class not knowing how to bring myself back to Earth. On several occasions, my teacher had asked me a question that I barely knew the answer to even though I knew the information was lodged somewhere in my brain. Thank God for textbooks or else I would not have retained anything in any of my classes. It was reading that was the only thing keeping my grades afloat, at least afloat enough for my standards. They were slipping below the line that kept me in the four-point-five range with nineties or ninety ones in everything except gym which was an easy A regardless. All I had to do was show up. That and my foreign language class was easy because she was there to help me and choir was just the struggles with music theory that realistically nobody understood. My average grade for my classes dropped from a ninety-eight to a ninety-three and I was not letting myself live it down. My physics teacher pulled me aside after class.

"Everything okay, Sarah?" She placed a hand on my

shoulder.

"Yeah. I'm doing okay."

"Trouble at home again?"

"No, nothing like that," I said, shaking my head.

"Okay," she said. "You just seem distracted is all."

"Really, I'm fine." From there, she let me on my way.

My next, and last, class of the day was gym, and I was not prepared for it, despite having my schedule changed to avoid the cheerleaders. We were nearing the end of the school year which meant that everything from here on out was all health knowledge and preparing for our max day. Sam tended to keep me in check there. She was the one who helped me with a lot in that class, helping me get stronger physically. In return, I helped her keep her grades above a D average. The locker room was already packed with pompous bitches, but that did not stop Sam from standing out. She was starting to look like one of those female bodybuilders, but without the steroids and nasty veins popping out everywhere.

"Sarah! Over here! Check it out!" I weaved through the crowd of girls making my way toward her and, as soon as I got to her, she shoved a shirt in my face holding it open to show me its back:

Samantha "The Annihilator" Jones
16

"Oh god…"

"Right? They turned out great! I've got 'em for all of my family, one for you, and one for Andrea." She pulled out a second shirt and handed the two of them to me. "You guys can wear them tonight at the game! You guys are coming, right?"

"Well yeah! It's the last game of the season."

"Awesome! Oh, hurry! Get changed! The robot is making her rounds."

Today was a track day. Not terrible for me, I was not the slowest girl in the class, but I was not the fastest either. No one was the fastest with Sam in the class with us. I tended to stay just behind Sam on track days. First half hour, we ran our mile times. The rest of the hour was cone drills. I hated it, but it was the only class I could constantly think about Andrea and not have to worry about missing something too important. The whistle sounded and I started running side by side with Sam at the lead.

*

Andrea's car always smelt so nice. She had a strawberry tree hanging on the rearview mirror and another pack of six sitting in the center console. Her car was kept immaculate to say the least and I mean it was damn near picture perfect from the day she got it. The only thing that it had lost was that new car smell, but I liked the smell of strawberries more. It gave me something to think about other than the fact that, for the last couple hours, I was not paying any attention to anything but Andrea. Not the game, Sam's performance in the game, or even whether or not we won. I was clueless. Thankfully, Sam was not mad at me for not paying attention. She knows I have never been a big sports person, but I always went just so I could cheer her on.

The three of us were on our way to our favorite froyo place downtown. It was a hot meet up for everyone… well, for those of us outcasts it was. Sam and I would go all the time, but Andrea had only been with us maybe two times before the night of the game because of cheer practice. All the same, I was glad she was

111

coming with us. We got in and ordered our usuals; Sam got her boba sorbet, Andrea got her strawberry chocolate swirl, and I got my peanut butter cheesecake.

"So…" Sam began, her mouth full of froyo, "how have you guys been? You know with the whole…" She trailed off and waved her spoon between us like we were hiding something. Andrea took my hand in hers.

"We've been good," she says, giving my hand a gentle squeeze. I wanted to melt like the froyo in my cup already was under the shop lights. It was getting hot under all those layers of clothes, and I did not think it was from the heat in the room. Sam flashed the two of us a big grin.

"Good! If anyone causes you two any trouble, make sure to tell me and I'll be sure to put them in their place!" She cracked her knuckles and her neck which only made us giggle. Sam was truly a force to be reckoned with when it came to our battles at school.

At some point, Andrea took my hand, and I made sure to let her know I noticed. We sat like that the rest of the evening as we joked and laughed. Our heads turned toward the door when the bell rang, and we caught sight of three bleach blonde heads come bobbing inside. They were headed toward the counter but made a detour to visit with us at our table. I went to pull my hand away from Andrea but she held on tight. My hand was trembling but it settled when she gave it a reassuring squeeze. They approached us with hands on hips like the kinds of girls you saw in teenage movies.

"Evening, girls… Sarah." Ouch. "What brings you three here?" Andrea, and I froze.

"Enjoying some victory froyo," she took in a big spoonful. "Why are you here?"

112

"Oh," she leaned slightly back and crossed her arms, "just picking up to sooth a sweet tooth before heading over to Connie's party."

"Oh really?" Sam asked. *Why are you leading them on?* is what I wanted to say, but I stayed silent.

"Yeah, you know, popular kids, booze. Way more fun than spending time with this loser." She nodded toward me. Ouch, number two. Andrea slammed a fist into the table.

"Will you three piss off already?" I flinched away from her and saw in her eyes an anger that I had never seen before, even the girls harassing us took a double take.

The one talking to us, supposedly the so-called leader of the three, flipped her hair and turned on her heel. A silent gesture to signal that they were leaving. The other two followed close on her heels while their shorts rode up on their asses.

"Way to stay classy, Tiffany!" Sam hollered at them followed by a catcall. All three of them pulled down the hems of their shorts.

Silence fell over the table again as we sat there trying to figure out what the hell just happened. First off, I felt like I was shaking in my seat and I noticed my hand had involuntarily gone slack in Andrea's. Second, Sam egging them on in the end was kind of funny. She seemed to be the only one of us who still had the nerve to shoot back at them. Thirdly, Andrea... wait, when did she hang her head? I rested my other hand on her shoulder and tried to look her in the eye. I wanted to ask if she was okay but it came out:

"Where in the hell did that come from?"

Andrea shook her head. "I have no idea. I just... they were making fun of you... then I just... I don't know... blew up."

"Well," Sam began, her mouth still full of froyo, "whatever

113

it was, was fucking awesome! I never thought you had it in ya."
She paused a moment. "It was a little startling though." I looked
at Andrea and she gave me a weak smile.

"Sorry if I scared you," she said. There was not anything for
me to say. Andrea had stood up to them for us and it made me
happy to see that she was not embarrassed to be with me, kind of
like the time she punched Rebecca in the face. I rested my head
back on her shoulder and closed my eyes. It was the first time in
a while I felt safe. She let go of my hand to put her arm around
me and began playing with my hair. I could fall asleep like that.

"Aww... get a room..." Sam chuckled when I flipped her
off for her remark then we went back to our evening.

The three of us piled into Andrea's car at the end of the night
so we could go home, though I did not want to go back to my
mother and her *plaything* as Sam liked to call him. Andrea drove
with one hand on the wheel and the other on the gear shift where
I let my hand rest on top of hers. Sam was playing with the aux
cable and constantly changing the song until she found one that
she wanted to listen to instead of the one she picked twenty
seconds before. I could not help but chuckle at her as she
continued to argue with herself over her music decisions. Our
light turned green and we started to move when I heard the
screeching tires.

*

I opened my eyes into a brightly lit room, and I could smell
the heavy disinfectants that were used on my surroundings. My
eyes focused on a clear line that went from the top of my hand,
up my arm, and finally up a silver stand where a clear plastic
bag hung on its hook. I was in the hospital, again, but I did not

114

know which one this time. I tried to move to sit up but quick pains shot through my arms and I fell back against the bed. My eyes slowly adjusted to the bright light from the ceiling, and I could make out the patterns in the tiles above my head. Outside my door, I could hear talking and either a radio or a TV turned to a news report. I could not make out what so, I partially listened in on the talking.

"How was your date last night?"

"It was going well until I got called in."

"Well, that sucks."

"Just one of the perks of being an on-call nurse. One of the girls is a friend of my daughter's though."

"So, you got called in for the accident then, huh?"

"Yeah. Nasty hit and run accident. It's all over the news right now." I tried to listen to what she was talking about, but I could still not make anything out from the static. "Good morning, sweetie." One of the nurses from the hall had come into my room with a clear bag like the one on the stand in her hands.

"Hi." My voice sounded like a frog. "What happened? Where am I?" The nurse smiled at me while she changed the bag.

"You were in a car accident but you only got a couple cuts and bruises. Maybe a concussion."

"Car accident?" I thought back and tried to rack my brain for anything that happened between the night prior and waking.

I could remember the game. I remembered going out with Sam and Andrea and running into the girls that we had told off when they were bothering us. We got in the car to go home. Andrea drove and Sam was messing with the radio. Then, it all came back in a stream. The tire screeching, the collision, the disorienting spinning, and the smell of burning rubber before everything went black. Why does it always turn to black?

"Where's Andrea?" I needed to see her but the sudden change in the nurse's face told me that was not going to happen soon. Her face dropped from that calming smile to a sort of sadness.

"Your friend is in another area getting treated. She was injured a bit more than you were."

"When can I see her?" Again, her face dropped.

"Family only for now, sweetie. I'm sorry." I nodded and let her get back to what she was doing.

The room went silent after she left, and all I could do was think about what happened. I held my own hands and tried to pretend that she was holding them, but I could tell that it was not her. I closed my eyes and tried to go back to sleep. The only thing better about this is that the bed I was in was more comfortable than my mattress and I would rather have the background noise of the hospital than the constant screaming, yelling, and fucking of my mother's house. It was the soundest sleep I could ever think of having, lying in a hospital bed. But no matter how much I tried to rest and no matter how long I kept my eyes closed, there was nothing to shut off the images from that night as they continued to play over and over again in my head. There was nothing to drown out the screaming. Eventually, I was finally able to stare simply at the back of my eyelids and rest.

*

Sam had an arm under me to help me walk. It still hurt to put pressure on my left leg. We were on our way over to see Andrea and, from what we had been told, she was still in a coma from the head trauma caused by the accident. Bruises and cuts lined the left side of her face from where the window had shattered.

Her leg was wrapped in a thick cast and raised, hanging by cords rigged to a pulley system. A mask covered her face feeding air into her lungs from a tube in the wall. I did not want to believe what I was looking at. I reached out to her to hold her hand and try to let her know that I was there, but it was short lived, and I did not get the chance to talk to her or to ask her to stay strong.

"Who let you in?" An older woman with greying black hair stood up in between me and Andrea's bed. "Excuse me, miss? Who let you in?" I tried to speak but the words were caught in my throat.

"We're friends of Andrea's and we wanted to see her," Sam tried explaining.

"Well, not today. As far as I am concerned, you two are the ones who were with her when this shit happened! You two are the ones who had kept her out late at night allowing for this to happen!" The woman looked at me. "I know who you are, Miss Cranston, and I have already gotten into contact with your mother." She took a breath. "In my household, and in the Lord's household, we do not take kindly to someone like you and I do not appreciate you bringing your filthy, disgusting sins into my household and tainting my daughter's good faith. Now leave!" I dropped my head at her words. *Filthy, disgusting, sin.* They hurt, because she was telling me I had hurt Andrea. I guess she was right.

"Who in the *fuck* do you think you are?" I looked at Sam as she started yelling at Andrea's mother. "This girl right here," she pointed at me, "happens to be someone who cares about your daughter very much and vice versa."

"You, shut up, and take that thing out of here with you before I call the authorities for talking to me the way that you are." Sam went to open her mouth again, but I gave her a squeeze on the elbow and shook my head at her. She hesitated a moment, but eventually we turned and walked away from Andrea and her mother.

*

I did not own a black dress so I stood back and away from the crowd with Sam and I was wearing black jeans and my black hoodie. Andrea's father had threatened to call the cops and tell them that we were harassing the family. They said we did not have a right to be there and that we were not invited. In more ways than one, they had a point. I had no right to be there, and I still felt guilty for what happened. It took Sam multiple attempts at talking to me about it to even get me to consider going. I did not want to be there and my hands were numb around the flowers I brought with me. It may have been the only chance I got to give any to her.

We hung back until everyone else had left and then we made our way over. As I got closer, I felt my feet get heavier. I did not want to see the coffin they had picked out for her, but I had a feeling that I knew. We looked down at the polished wooden case. They picked the cherrywood, her favorite stain color. I leaned down and set the flowers on top then folded my hands in front of me.

"How are you feeling?" Sam asked. I was sad, she knew that, but I knew what she was asking.

My breath caught in my throat, and I shook my head at her. It hurt to breathe as I tried to pull back the tears, but I could not. Sam put her arm around my shoulder and pulled me in as I started to cry. Not crying necessarily for myself, but crying more for her, for her family. This was the second person I have seen buried in my life, but I did not get the chance to cry the last time.

Here Without You

They held an annual memorial for Andrea at school during the winter assembly. Sam and I sat in the front row of the bleachers watching as the JROTC group brought out and presented the wreath for the picture of her that stood next to the podium. Following them was a presentation from the school choir and orchestra as they performed a version of *Amazing Grace* that brought more than half the room to tears. I continued to sit there on the plastic bench with a massive lump in my throat that I kept trying to choke back. Sam kept my hand in hers and squeezed any time she thought I might be faltering.

"Thank you," I whispered to her.

"You're welcome," she said, wiping tears of her own from her face.

"Thank you all for your continued support of the Marks family," our principal said, her voice amplified by the podium's microphone. The bell rang to end second period. "You are all dismissed, please make your way to your third period classes." The gym erupted into sound as everyone got up and made their way out.

I stood up and gave Sam a hug. "I'll see you later?"

"Yeah," she said, giving my hand one last squeeze, then making her way out with everyone else.

I looked around the gym trying to find them. They had to be there after the eulogy that our principal gave with the gesture to the other side of the gymnasium. I remember meeting them once, and I remember them being highly religious. Somewhere in the back of my head, I doubted that they remembered me at all, but I still wanted to see them and maybe provide closure for them or even myself. I felt guilty being the last one to see her alive.

The two of them were talking to our principal and had their backs to me, but it was hard to dismiss her mother. From the back, the woman looked exactly like Andrea, but with hints of grey in her otherwise black hair. The principal had just finished talking to them by the time I had reached the triage. I circled around so that I did not address them from behind.

"Mister and Misses Marks?"

"Yes, child? What do you want?" Her mother was every bit authoritative as she was gentle in her tone.

"Sarah Cranston," I said, holding out my hand. "I was not sure if you guys would remember me but..."

"We remember you All right," Mister Marks said with a low growl. "And we don't much care to be talking to you."

"I just wanted to say how sorry I am for your loss." The words came out in a rush, and I felt the need to shy away. Misses Marks stood tall and got up in my face, or down in my face in this sense.

"We don't need your pity!" she barked. "We don't want your pity, and we don't want you talking to us! It is the fault of your sins that lost us our daughter! It is you who corrupted her and gave her that fate! Leave our family in peace, before we decide to exorcise the demons in you that make you this way!" She turned and walked away in a huff with her husband close on her heels.

I stood there and watched them storm out of the gymnasium. Everyone thought it, they told me every day in the looks that they would give me and the snide remarks that I heard whispered behind my back. It was different this time, though. It was the first time someone had said it to my face as angrily and as blunt. A living sin or blemish in the purity of humankind. I never went to church, and I never took any interest in any of its teachings, but I felt like their display of disgust was something embedded in their minds.

The one-minute bell rang for the start of the third period, but I did not feel like going to class and the gym seemed too empty and cold. Instead, I went to the one place where I knew I could hide safely; the library. All the way across campus, tucked into the corner between the office and the history hall. Miss Levey watched me walk in and was quick to hand me an access key for one of the computer terminals. I sat and worked on my English paper.

Silence in the library was one of the best things in the world. It was calming, it was peaceful, and the only disruption to the silence was the clacking of the keyboard and the occasional flipping of the pages of the books. I hid there during the third period, lunch, fourth period, and fifth period before someone finally came to check on me. My English paper was one concluding paragraph to being completed when I felt the hand land on my shoulder. I dropped my hands from the keyboard and lowered my head with a sigh.

"How long?" I asked her. The words were heavy on my lips.

"About four hours. The day is almost over." It was my guidance counselor. "Did you get any work done?" she asked

"My English paper is almost done," I said with a shrug.

"When is it due?"

"Two weeks. I have my history paper that's close to done too. I was gonna work on that when I was done with this one."

"You know you missed out on all the study guides for your

finals?"

"Yeah, I know. I don't need them though." I moved the mouse and clicked on the save icon for my paper, and was prepared to close the computer down when she spoke up again.

"How about I write you a pass for today, and you go ahead and get those assignments finished. I already have the study guides from the classes you missed as well as the one from your last class." She placed a folder in front of me that had several stapled packets inside. "Okay?"

"Okay," I said. "Thank you," I mumbled.

"You're very welcome. I know how hard it has been for you, but you've still managed to get your work done and keep your grades up." She paused for a moment. "I have to ask, are you struggling to reach the top spot in your class, or are you purposefully avoiding it?"

"Well," I started with a chuckle. "That is partly because of gym class. I'm not as strong as anyone else in the class, and it keeps me just on that threshold."

"Have you ever thought about dropping gym and working toward the number one spot and maybe being valedictorian?"

"Number three is fine with me," I said. "I was never one for public speaking anyway."

"Fair enough." She dropped her hand from my shoulder. "Good luck with your assignments."

"Thank you." I looked up at her and smiled my first smile in what felt like weeks.

She walked out of the library and left me to my work. The computer was still open on my English paper, and I began working on it again. Why I decided to do a final project on Jane Austen was beyond me, but I worked on it anyway and struggled the entire way through. At least seven hours went into working on the paper alone, and none of that included reading her work or doing any of the research. It took the rest of the day to get it done and fill in all of my citations. The final bell of the day rang in the library, and I closed up the documents and the computer terminal. I handed Miss Levey the computer access key and she looked at me.

"Are you sure you're doing All right?" she asked.

"No," I said, shaking my head. "But I don't have much of a choice."

"No one is forcing you to be okay," she said. "I remember the days you would come in here and work on your assignments until Andrea came to take you home. She was special to you. I know that much, and it's okay for you to be sad. Just never give up, okay?" I nodded. "I'll see you on Monday."

"See you Monday." I waved goodbye and left through the office.

Sam was waiting for me by the flagpole with her hand gripping her hair at the roots in her scalp while holding one of her study guides in the other. If she gripped any tighter, she might start pulling her own hair out. I snuck up behind her and peered around her arm at the guide in her hand. It was easy basic-level algebra and stuff that I could do in a matter of seconds, but she looked like she was going to rip the guide in half with how frustrated she was getting.

"If you want, I can help you study this weekend." She jumped.

"Damnit, Sarah!" she yelped. "You about made me smack the shit out of you."

"Sorry," I said with a giggle.

"You may be small, but being sneaky like that is just downright Satanic!" There was that reference again. I frowned

123

and gripped my bag with both hands. "Hey, are you okay?"

"Yeah, I'm fine," I lied. I hoped the redness in my cheeks did not give me away.

"Are you doing anything this evening?" she asked.

"No, nothing. Why?"

"You, me, and the mall! What do you say?" I looked at her and saw the wide grin she had on her face.

"Sure," I said. She squealed and wrapped me up in a bear hug that lifted me up off the ground. "But only if you agree to study with me this weekend!" I gasped.

"Ugh, fine! We can study tomorrow. But tonight, we seize the day!" She grabbed me by the hand and dragged me along to the closest bus stop near the school.

*

The mall was packed practically from wall to wall. Everyone was weaving in and out of one another as were Sam and I, but she never let go of my arm. She did well in keeping her and I together where everyone else was moving like a stampede of wild cows. Mothers with their small children, teens with their groups, boys, and girls, with their partners. It made me anxious being around so many people. The last time I was at the mall was with Andrea, and she had me distracted enough to be able to flow through the crowd with her without feeling cornered in a box.

Sam dragged me into a hair salon that was as close to packed inside as it was outside in the rest of the mall. Several women were getting their hair done in the chairs and had big tinted domes placed over their heads. Almost the same number were having strands of their hair wrapped up in tin foil strips. One of the stylists came up to the two of us with one of the most pompous looks I had seen. This salon was not cheap, and the way the stylists acted proved the point.

"Can I help you two?" she asked. I could not tell if she hated her job, or was disgusted by us coming into such a high-end place.

"I have an appointment," Sam chimed arrogantly. It was weird seeing her act so up-tight.

"Name," she sighed.

"Samantha Jones."

"Very well, we'll call you when we're ready." She walked away and Sam pulled me to the side where we sat on a bench to wait.

"Why are we here?" I asked.

"We're here to get our hair done, and you're not allowed to ask questions about what you're getting." That made me nervous.

"Why?" I asked, feeling my anxiousness grow.

"Because," she gave me a slight nudge with her shoulder. "If I told you, you wouldn't have come with me."

"I'm not sure I really want to be here anyway." I looked around at the ceiling tiles. "I feel like I'm going to be sick."

"You are going to be fine, and you're going to look great!" she said. She pulled out her half of our necklace. "You can trust me." I pulled out my half and put it close enough to link with hers. The magnets were weak, but they still pulled on one another to make their perfect circle.

The women in the salon worked on my hair for what felt like hours, but it was really only an hour and a half. Sam was done in half the time getting highlights done in her hair and the sides shaved down again, but she only had one side shaved this time. The other side she draped over the opposite end. I was still wrapped in the foil strips and waiting for them to come take them

125

out and rinse my hair. Sam sat down in the chair next to me.

"How do you feel, legs?" I looked at her.

"I'm feeling like you should have forgotten that nickname considering you haven't called me that in so long." I looked up at her and saw her huge grin. It scared me.

"Oh, I'll never forget that day," she said. "I will always remember the day that someone almost outran me, and I think you have a couple of times. What was your fastest mile time this semester?"

"Just under five and a half I think?" I tried to remember, but it was something that I never really cared about enough to remember. They told me to run, so I would run and push as hard as I could.

"Yeah, you outran me by twenty-three seconds." She nudged me in the arm.

"All right." One of the hair stylists came back. "I think you are just about done here." She started to take the foil out of my hair. Each strand came loose in a deep, dark red. The only color that came to mind was auburn. I looked at Sam through the mirror.

"What did you have them do?" I could not hide the shock in my voice or my face.

"Like your running, I thought you could use a change of pace. Best way to forget the past is to outrun it completely." She patted me on the shoulder once the stylist was gone.

"I don't know whether to be happy with it or mad you had it done."

"It looks good, doesn't it? It makes your eyes pop!"

She was right, the color did make my eyes pop. It made everything pop with how pale I was. I went to run a hand through it, but stopped knowing they had not rinsed it, and I would have just stained my hands. The sight of it put so many different thoughts into my head. It looked great, but what was my mother going to say to me? What was she going to do to me? What was *he* going to do to me? I did not want to think about it. My mind shifted to Andrea and I saw her in the mirror in front of me.

"I love the new look," her reflection said. She was still beautiful, and the thought of her put a sad smile on my face as well as warm tears in my eyes.

"Thank you," I replied in a hoarse whisper.

I watched Sam walk up and replace her. The smile on her face was soft and caring. She put a hand on my shoulder, and I reached up to hold it. We looked at each other in the mirror and I saw that we both had tears in our eyes. Andrea was as good a friend to Sam as she was to me, and I know her passing weighed as heavily with Sam as it did with me. We were both there the night she died and we both woke up in the same hospital that she died in.

I kept replaying the accident in my head. Over and over and over I heard the tires screeching and the metal crunching from the weight of the impact. I was thrown side to side and given a concussion from hitting my head against the driver side glass. The hand that was holding Andrea's was broken as was my wrist. My airbags never went off. Sam got tossed around the back seat and broke her arm. They said if she was not wearing her seatbelt, she would have been thrown from the car. Andrea took the full force of the front and side airbags, but the junk car that hit us splintered, and part of the frame punched through the shattered window, punctured the airbag, and struck her in the head. The cause of death was blunt force trauma. To make matters worse, the guy that hit us spent two days in the hospital, seven nights in prison, and got a slap on the wrist after his insurance agency paid for the extent of the total damages to us and the car. I wondered what he would think about my hair and if he would recognize me if he saw me.

Sam paid the stylists and we walked out of the salon, I walked out feeling different from before. It felt like there were so many eyes on me. I kept looking around thinking that everyone was looking at me, but there were only about five or six in total. People still avoided me, thinking I was younger than thirteen. No one would have guessed that I was seventeen with how small I was. I was convinced Sam's chest was larger than my head.

We sat down at the mall's pizza place that had unfortunately changed hands over the years. At least they still had a pizza that we would eat. I liked eating salads, but once they put the veggies on the pizza, it was ruined. The same went for pineapple. I hated it and wished it never existed to begin with. Sam and I silently made fun of everyone that we caught buying one of those monstrosities, but she shortly changed the subject after a couple of slices.

"So," she began. "Have you given any thought to our graduation?" she asked.

"Not really, no." I looked at her confused. "What is this about?"

"Let's face it, I'm not cut out for this. The whole school thing I mean. College might be different, but not this."

"What are you saying?"

"Well, since I turned eighteen last month, I was thinking about dropping out and getting my GED." I choked on my soda wishing she had waited until I was done drinking.

"Drop out?" I asked. "What about me? What about your sports?"

"My sports ended in winter, Sarah. There's nothing left for

me at that school and there weren't any offers for athletic scholarships." I looked at her, still dumbfounded and she looked back dejected. "I need to get out of that house. The sooner the better." The more she said it, the more it made sense to me, and the more I wanted a part of it. The thought came to me so suddenly that it shocked me.

"What if I came with you? The heavens know I need out of my house too." I looked her in the eye and reached for her hand. "Whatever we do, we do it together. I don't have anyone else I can trust or lean on."

"But what about your academics? You've got schools knocking down your door trying to get you to attend. I can't pull you away from all of that."

"You're not going to have to," I reassured her. "Like you said, schools are knocking down my door. I can go anywhere. Which means I can go anywhere you go." We looked at each other, eye to eye. She knew that I was certain with my choice just as I knew she was certain with hers.

"What about school?" she asked.

"I had the credits to graduate after last year. The only reason I stayed really was because I felt like I didn't have anywhere else to go. I felt like I couldn't go anywhere else." Sam nodded and looked down from me.

"We can do it tonight. My mother stopped caring about when I came home or if I did at all, so I've been staying with Brad. You can stay with us until we figure it out."

"Thank you, Sam." I felt the tears in my eyes again.

Leaving meant putting my past behind me. My mother, my stepfather, all of the abusers and bullies in the area that ever picked on me or beat me. It meant leaving behind Andrea and her memory, but it might be a memory I could carry with me. I fiddled with my half of the pendant around my neck and wished Andrea and I had gotten one like it for ourselves. Love only lasts so long as you can remember it, and even then, a memory is all it will ever be.

*

The whole house was dark when we pulled up and my mother's car was not in the driveway giving Brad all the space he needed to back his truck in. We were lucky he owed Sam a favor after taking her to a bad sushi restaurant where the two of them got terrible food poisoning. Having his truck made moving my room easy. It was mostly boxes packed full of books, and there was no taking the mattress or the bedding. As far as clothes went, I packed a suitcase with a week's worth of clothes and stuffed the rest into a single box, shoes and all. We barely loaded half of the bed of Brad's truck.

"This is it?" he asked.

"I don't come from much," I told him. "Be glad I worked summers in the library, or the suitcase would have been the only thing I packed."

"Makes me feel useful," he said with a shrug. "Are you sure about all of this, Sam?"

"As sure as anything. Don't worry, I'll do all the talking with your aunt and uncle. They love me!" She patted him on the side of his head, then kissed his cheek. What Brad saw in her was way beyond me.

"Let's go," I said. "I don't want to be here when she gets back."

The three of us loaded into his truck and made our way to the other side of town, the rich side of town, where he lived with his aunt and uncle. They owned a two-story house with a pool and a guest house both on the property. He claimed his uncle made his money as an officer in the Air Force flying planes for a living. It sounded like easy money to me, if it were not for the fact that I would never clear a physical. At least I did not think I could, not at my size.

He wheeled his truck around the back of the main house to the guest house garage. It was not the first time I had been on the property. Sam had brought Andrea and I here as her plus ones for his seventeenth birthday and I would never forget it. A pool party in the early fall. Way too cold for me to go swimming, but not for Andrea. She wore a two piece suit covered by a sheer black shawl. It was the most skin I had ever seen on her, and I dreaded every moment she kept it hidden under the water.

"Home sweet home!" Sam chimed, bringing me out of the memory. She hopped out of the truck and skipped inside.

"I'd ask you if she was always like this," Brad said, starring after her. "But it might ruin the mystery."

"Trust me," I began. "The more you actively try to understand Sam, the less you actually end up understanding." I walked into the living room and saw Sam already spread out on the couch with a bottle of soda in her hand.

"You want anything to drink?" she asked.

"Water is fine." She motioned to Brad and he moved through to the kitchen with a sigh.

"He is such a bottom," I said to Sam, taking the seat next to her.

"If you start sounding any more like me, people will think we're sisters."

"Not with this hair they won't." I played with the auburn red hair that now draped over my shoulders. "I should have had it

131

trimmed."

"Nonsense! Why cut off such beautiful hair?"

"I did at one point. Hacked it off in the shower myself."

"And you had every reason to." She grabbed my hand, and I leaned into her shoulder.

Brad came back with my water and a soda for himself, setting both on the table before taking the seat opposite Sam and putting an arm around her shoulder. I saw her prepare to make a snide remark, then reel it in and smile at him instead. It looked like she really liked him. I had half a mind to say that she loved him, and the other half to say he loved her. They were weird and they did not make sense, but they were cute.

The three of us stayed up watching sitcoms the rest of the night until the two of them fell asleep on the couch next to me. I sat in the dark, having turned the TV off, and listened to the crickets chirping outside. Deciding that I wanted to join them, I stepped out into the cold air. The lights in the pool gave off just enough to see my breath. I rolled up my pant legs and stuck my feet into the water. It was freezing, and I had to ease them in, inch by inch. I got them in and let out the breath that I was holding. There was a splash next to me and another set of feet were put dangling in the water. I looked up into Sam's eyes.

"Saw you walk out."

"I couldn't sleep," I told her. "I'm still trying to figure everything out."

"Well, we've got most of that figured out for you."

"What do you mean?" I asked.

"Brad talked to his aunt and uncle for you. They're willing to let you stay here for a little until you can get all of your school stuff figured out." She coughed to clear her throat. "Brad took up an offer in California to play for a college out there, and he asked

132

me to go with him. He's going out early to work with the team during the offseason."

"So, you guys are leaving me after all?" I looked down into the water.

"Only for a couple of weeks. It won't be long before we're all happy and comfortable in Cali." She scoffed. "Hell! We already have the whole apartment set up. Great little two bed, two bath place Brad's aunt and uncle have for us in a nice part of town."

"I don't know if I can do this," I said, my voice shaking. I was sure before and that was one thing, but being scared was something I did not expect to feel. Sam put her arm around my shoulder.

"Just think," she started. "Next year, you and I will have left this place behind us, and everyone who wronged us."

"I know. That's part of what I'm afraid of." The wind started to blow and I heard it whispering in the trees. Whispers of my past maybe, of everything I was ready to leave behind. I did not know if they trumped leaving Andrea behind.

Second Chance

I kept hearing from people that you only graduate from high school once and that I should savor every moment of it. My mother says I should be grateful because she never graduated and only got her GED three years after I was born. She told me that in between taking her pain meds and washing them down with a bottle of Jack. I was ready for one thing, the ability to go where I wanted. I had no intentions of going home after the ceremony and went straight to Brad's aunt and uncle's to grab my bag, my phone, and the wad of cash I had collected from working part time at the town library.

I left knowing that my mother was at the liberty of herself and her fuck toy that she called a husband. I was glad to know that all that was keeping her afloat was my granddad's retirement money. She did it to herself and to the people around her. Brad's aunt and uncle asked me if I wanted to go see her to say goodbye. I told them that there would be plenty of time to say goodbye in the end. They looked at me, puzzled, but I know what I meant. There would be plenty of time for goodbyes when she was dead.

I bought my ticket at the bus station for the bus that would take me all the way down the line to the coast. Two thousand miles from my home town to California where my mother will never be able to have a hold on me. A one-way trip for me to have another chance at a happy life. With my bag in my lap and nothing but the moon, I started my journey with a couple changes of clothes and a book knowing what was waiting for me.

*

I walked into the small two-bedroom apartment with my backpack and a small suitcase in hand. The key was under the welcome mat just like they said, and it made life easier than having to talk to the foreman to let me into the place. Just a quick look around gave the apartment the impression of poor first year college student life. A few small bits of furniture already sat in their respective places. A futon sat in the middle of the living room floor behind a birch-colored coffee table, both facing a small TV that sat on a stand of the same color. In the corner was a single desk with a chair, laptop, and recording mic with a screen still open to some low-tech video editing software. Just to the other end of the kitchen was a small folding table with matching chairs for a makeshift dining table. It looked cheap compared to the rich atmosphere, but I was happy. It was going to be a great home.

A blonde blur rushed me and wrapped me in a tight bear hug as soon as I set my bag down on the floor. A familiar scent of winter mint and strawberries filled my nose.

"OMG! I am so glad you made it!" Their arms were tight around my arms and back and it felt like they were going to crush my shoulders, but I did my best to return the embrace.

"It's good to see you too, Sam." It was hard to respond, having the air squeezed out of my lungs. It had been a while since I experienced one of her bear hugs. After a few moments of not being able to breathe properly, she finally let me go.

"So how was the trip up? You didn't run into any problems, did you?"

I shook my head. "Most of the time I was reading and, let

me tell you, two days on a bus feels like nothing when you've got good reading material."

"*Oooooo…* what'd you read?" I opened my backpack and pulled out the 464-page monster that took up half of the space.

"Grapes of Wrath." She gave me that 'really?' expression and I nodded. "I bought the book back in junior year as a birthday present for myself, but I never got the chance to read it. It was a shame though that I could not fit any more books that I saw on my trip into my bag." I held the book tight to my chest.

"I'm not so sure about that part," she said, giving me a concerned glance

"What do you mean?" Sam took me by the elbow and led me into the back hallway to the bedrooms where we turned right, went past the bathroom and into what I assumed was my room.

It was small but cozy and already completely furnished with a dresser, bed, nightstand, desk, and a bookshelf that went from the floor to the ceiling. It was not the room itself that had me impressed but the bookshelf that was practically filled from end to end with books. I was in shock at the sight and almost let the Steinbeck novel slip from my grasp. How much did all of this cost her? There were a lot of limited editions and leather bounds among them. I was able to recognize the books I had shipped with them as well.

"So," she began, "you like it?"

"I… Sam this is…"

"I know," she sighed. "It would have been completely full, but I figured you'd need room for your schoolbooks as well." I looked at her with a puzzled expression.

"What do you mean?"

"Oh yeah, I forgot to give this to you first." She pulled a slip of paper from her pocket. "I talked to my advisor and got you a meeting with her and the dean tomorrow morning." I looked between her and the paper in my hand. Sure enough, it had the dean's signature on it. "They said they've already been looking at your transcripts."

"You're kidding?" Sam shook her head. "Oh my God! Thank you!" I wrapped my arms around her neck a little more excitedly than I had intentioned, but it was worth giving one of her bear hugs back to her.

*

Both the dean and Sam's advisor were two of the nicest people I had ever met. Although they were not able to get me into the school for the semester, they said that they would look into my application once I had it in. The only issue is that my high school refused to give me records of my graduation and my transcripts without my mother's say so and, every time they tried to talk to her, she refused to cooperate. When it came time for my application to be due, I had everything I needed except my high school transcripts, and my application was ultimately rejected.

Sam talked me into getting a job that I ultimately did not want because of most of the experiences I had with people, but I took it and started as a waitress and it sucked. A job based solely on the tips I made was one of the worst things I could have done to myself. My first week, I brought home close to nothing because nobody was giving me any tips. Meanwhile, Sam kept bringing home check after check from the bar, but I was never really upset about that. She spent most of it on Brad, and I so we could go out and have fun every now and again.

There was one day Sam talked me into going to the gym and it took a lot of courage to get me into any form of gym clothes

137

that were not sweatpants and a hoodie. That was mainly in part to the fact that almost all of the girls at the gym, including Sam, were there in tight leggings and either crop tops or sports bras. They were showing off everything they had to offer and looking good doing it too. It made me uncomfortable.

Sam spent most of her time on the weight machines while I transitioned between the cardio and core exercises. While I was running on the treadmill, a woman approached me dressed in green shorts and a green shirt. She watched me for a moment before leaving me alone. I saw her again while I was in the stretching room doing some crunches, sit-ups, and planks. Finally, I saw her a third time when Sam pulled me over to do some more arm exercises with her. Sam had forced me to do pullups and that was when I felt like I was being watched more adamantly. It was strange and, when we left, there was a flyer in the windshield of Brad's truck. I pulled it out and looked at the front of it to see that it was a flyer for the Marine Corps.

"They must have loved you in there," I said showing it to Sam and she gave it a look over.

"Oh yeah, I know this girl. She's one of the instructors at the university." She handed it back to me.

"Instructor?"

"Yeah, one of the ROTC instructors. I didn't know she did recruiting as well. It would explain why she tried to get in touch with me so often." Sam got in the truck and I followed suit.

I kept looking over the flyer in my hand reading each section. The part that caught my eye the most was the section on education benefits. I could really use it to help get an edge and, maybe, they would be able to get ahold of my transcripts. I looked back at Sam.

"Do you think I could tag along with you tomorrow

138

morning?"

"Sure." She thought about it a moment. "Wait, you're not actually considering *that* as an option, are you?" I shrugged and she shook her head. "You do you, legs. I'll help you and support you, but I don't like the idea."

The next morning, Sam took me with her to the university and I made my way timidly to the building that housed the ROTC instructors. They made it easy to identify with the military flag flying on the flagpole. Walking up the stairs of the building did not ease my nerves at all. Every person I walked past was either in a really nice uniform or dressed in a dark green blocky camouflage. They stared at me, and I could not blame them. I looked like I did not belong at all wearing a pair of jeans and a Pink Floyd shirt.

There was a row of chairs sitting outside the office and they looked more like rest areas for students to wait for their classes to start. I glanced into the office and it looked like there was not anyone inside so I took a seat in one of the chairs. Other students continued to shuffle by and stare at me as they went past. Some were in uniforms, the others were dressed kind of like me, and in that they were dressed nothing like me. I just did not know how to describe someone not in uniform. To ignore them, I pulled a book out of my bag and began reading. A fantasy novel that Sam thought that I might enjoy reading. Every now and again, I looked up at the people passing by to see if I recognized anyone. No one came by. Eventually, I just went back to my book and ignored the people that passed by. After a while, I looked up because I felt like someone was walking toward me directly and it turned out to be Sam.

"You're still waiting?" She asked. I nodded. "I tried to text you to see where you were at."

"You did?" I pulled out my phone to see a missed call and a couple of text messages from Sam. "Oops… sorry." She shrugged.

"It's all right." I stood up and put my book back in my bag. Sam and I started to walk away when someone caught our attention.

"Oh, you made it." We both turned around. "Hey, Sam. Come to finally sign up or…"

"It's still a no from me, Jennifer."

"Oh well," Jennifer said with a shrug. She walked toward us and held a hand out to me. "Sergeant Jennifer Martin."

"Sarah." I shook her hand. She was in a blue and tan uniform instead of the green workout clothes I saw her in the other day.

"Nice to finally meet you, Sarah. Come on in." Jennifer walked back and held the door open for me. I looked at Sam, and she gestured for me to go ahead and gave me a thumbs up for reassurance. The knot in my stomach and the lump in my throat told me otherwise.

The meeting with Jennifer was as much of a stereotypical interview as it was understanding where I would fit in with the Marines. Part of my advantage was my weight in line with my height. Apparently being just over five foot and weighing over one ten made me a valuable asset in fitness standards. I always knew I was fast; I did not know it was because I was tiny. That combined with my practice ASVAB scores, I could potentially qualify for just about anything. The only issue is that I had no idea what I wanted to do. With that, I left the office with a stack of papers to sign and an understanding of what was expected of me. Sam was waiting for me when I walked out.

"About time," she scoffed jokingly. "How was it?" I showed her the stack of papers.

140

"I have to get these signed before I do anything else, but according to Jennifer, it's looking pretty good for me."

"So, are you going to do it?"

"I don't know yet." I looked at the stack of papers in my hand before putting them in my bag. "One of the issues is I don't have any references that I can use."

"How many do you need?"

"Twelve."

"Jesus..." Sam was quiet for a bit. "Well, I'm sure we'll get it figured out."

When Sam and I got home, I set the papers down on the desk in my room. I stayed there for a while looking them over and thinking about what I really wanted to do. After a while, I got a call from home. It was a number I did not recognize but I answered it anyway.

*

I sat there in a cemetery in San Diego dressed in black, but actually wearing a dress this time. The navy uniforms marched past me as they carried my dad to his final resting place. It was where he was raised, it was where he trained, it was where he was stationed, and now it was where he was buried. They handed me a triangle folded flag and had a line of seven soldiers fire off three shots each. The flag I placed on my desk, and I noticed the Marine Corps papers finished but unsigned. I turned them into Jennifer the next morning.

My mother called me three times while I was out. I chose to ignore each one of them. She left me a voice mail after the third, then tried sending me a drunken text that was not even readable from the jumbled-up mess she had all the letters in. I managed to make out the words *hi* and *dick* and that was just about it. I told Sam about it and her exact words were "Fuck that bitch!" Sam and I went out that night for her birthday and we were enjoying bowling with a couple of her friends who would sneak her a drink every now and then when the attendants were not paying us any attention. Some old woman snuck up on us and started talking to us like she knew us, but I could not understand a word between the slurs in her voice, and I could not see her because of how dark it was in the bowling alley. We ignored her and continued our game until the lights came up, and I finally caught sight of the woman who had been stalking us and it was like I was looking into a mirror that aged me thirty years. How she found us was beyond me.

"Hello, Sarah." I looked between her and Sam several times. Sam just shrugged and her friends had that *Who the fuck is this chick?* look on their faces.

I pulled my mother by the arm away from the group and sat her down away from the others in the dining area by the snack stand. She was swaying back and forth in her chair and it looked like she was about to actually fall out of it. Her hair was a mess and her face looked sunken in and was highlighted by her pale skin. She looked sick like she was going to pass out there at the table. If I was being honest with myself, I should have sat back a little further from the table to make sure she did not get any vomit on me, but I held my ground, leaned back in my chair, and crossed my arms.

"What do you want?" I asked her.

"Not even a 'hello?'"

"No." She gave me a sinister look.

"You had me worried sick you little brat. I deserve a little more respect."

142

"What you deserve is a kick in the ass and a coffee to sober you up," I mumbled. She reached across the table to try and smack me but she fell short and faceplanted into the wood polish.

"You little bitch." I waved down a server and he almost told me my mother had been cut off before I ordered her the coffee. Then he understood and went away.

"What are you doing here?" She stared at me.

"I'm here to bring you home, Sarah."

"I *am* home."

"With who? Your whore friend and her clan of bimbos?"

"The only whore here is you, and you're a drunk one at that." I stood up from the table. "I am already tired of talking to you." I pulled out a five for the server and handed it to him when he brought the coffee. "Find your way home, but mine is not with you." She grabbed my hand as I tried to walk away, but I jerked it away and she fell sprawling onto the floor.

"You are nothing without me!" She yelled.

"No, I am stronger without you," I said, and I walked away from her.

Sam tried to stop me as she was making her way over to check on us but I shouldered past her and stormed outside into the dimly lit parking lot. I could hear the cars rolling past on the street and the faint sound of sirens in the distance. Looking up to the moon, I let out a deep breath and watched the air from my lungs cloud above my head. I sat down on the front step and put my head in my hands. My eyes watered and the lump formed in my throat but I fought back the sobs that threatened to leave my barred lips. After a while, I felt someone sit down beside me and put their arm around my shoulder.

"Hey, Sam."

"You okay?" I nodded at her. "You wanna talk about it?" I

143

shook my head. "Okay, let's go home then."

Sam and I said good night to her friends and made our way home. Everything was quiet by the time we arrived and we both marched up the stairs and closed ourselves in our rooms. I laid there in my bed quietly, thinking about my mother, and if I should have stayed longer to talk with her. No, I was the stronger person by not letting her get to me, but I did not think I got my point across to her that I was expecting. My phone went off over a dozen times throughout the night and it was all from the same number. Sleep was hard to come by, and I did not really sleep at all. When I woke up, I had two voice mails; one from my mother, and another from an unknown number. The one from my mother was basically her cussing me out for leaving her at the bowling alley and also for not answering my phone. One, she was drunk. Two, it was the middle of the night and I did not have the energy to deal with her.

The second was from someone who brought up that my mother was in the hospital and that I was the emergency contact listed for her. Something about her kidneys, and I assumed it was her alcoholism. Part of me was concerned, the other was understanding that she had it coming after all these years. She died a week later because both kidneys failed, and I was not a viable donor despite being her daughter. I was glad to see her gone and to watch her coffin be lowered down next to dad's. It was the least I could do. I did not inherit any money from her and could not afford to send her body home. Sam's sister paid for the funeral and the plot. I did not bother to cry and the first thing I did, having her gone, was request my transcripts from high school and finally finish my application.

I had to retract my military papers after that and get a fresh copy to fill out and sign which took a lot longer than I wanted to.

Sam asked why I did it and I told her that I had changed my mind about joining. She was none the wiser. I did not tell her that they had to be redone because I was in the process of legally changing my name. I felt like I did not have any ties to my mother anymore and decided to drop her name 'Cranston' and take Dad's name instead. I became 'Sarah Jane Palmer,' permanently erasing and rewriting who I was.

Hurt

I walked down the street from the bus stop where Sam said she was going to meet me. It took me forever walking up and down the street to find it, especially after realizing that it was across the street from where I started. The discount furniture store was anything but extravagant. Everything looked like it had crawled out of the seventies or eighties with all of the different floral designs that they had as well as the god-awful colors. The first one that caught my attention was something like a seafoam green covered in flowers like the ones from my dad's baby pictures when he would show them to me. As I continued to look around, I saw that nothing in the store really matched the look in the rest of the apartment.

"Sarah! Over here!" I looked up and saw Sam standing on the other side of the store trying to wave me over. The fact that she was screaming all the way across the store was embarrassing. I walked over to her and she threw an arm around me. "I was starting to think you wouldn't show."

"It's my apartment too," I said. "Besides, without me, who knows what you'll show up with."

"My taste isn't that bad!" she whined.

"Tell that to the blue bookcases and orange tables. It looks like the Broncos mascot exploded in there." Sam raised her hand in protest, but I saw the thought die on her lips.

"Yeah, fair point," she said defeated. "In my defense, we had to do something when Brad's aunt and uncle took back the

146

furniture they bought."

"Come on," I said. "Let's see if we can find something black, or white, and get some sense of normal in the apartment."

The two of us circled the sales floor looking at what felt like hundreds of different couches. Each one was uniquely different, and a lot of them would not fit in the apartment. Even the ugly brown leather reclining couch she tried to convince me to let her get. Several holes told me it was falling apart at the seams and was an even bigger 'no' than the green floral couch. We spent half an hour looking at and sitting on old couches until we saw one that would work; a three seated white couch that was plenty big for the three of us side by side, but not so big that it would go from the wall to the bar of the kitchen.

"This one seems nice," I said. I sat down on it and sank in comfortably. The cushions were soft, but not so soft that it made me want to fall asleep instantly like my mattress. Sam flopped down right beside me and rested her head on my shoulder.

"Yeah, this one seems appropriate."

"You guys finding everything okay?" One of the salesmen crept up on us while we were not paying any attention.

"Yes, actually. I think we are going to take this one!" I chimed while giving him a big smile.

"Wonderful! I'll go ring it up and mark it as 'sold' so the other customers don't try and take it from you. If you ladies will follow me?" We got up and followed him to the register. Sam glanced at me.

"He's kind of cute," she whispered.

"Seriously?" I asked. "I look at one guy who makes me blush and now you point out every guy we meet?"

"It's not my fault you haven't met anyone since we came out here!"

147

"I didn't come out here to meet anyone. I came out here to go to class and get good grades and get my degree."

"Then what's with the recruitment paperwork?" she asked. I stopped and looked at her. "It was on the desk under the laptop, love. I thought you retracted it?"

"Damnit," I muttered.

"What's going on with you?" she asked.

"Look," I said. "I'm just trying to figure everything out still. It's just something that I've been thinking about."

"Is that why you're sneaking out at five in the morning too?"

"Maybe..." We got up to the register. "Look, can we talk about this later? Please?"

"Fine," she said.

"So," the salesman began. "Where can I have this shipped to?"

*

I sat on the bus hoping that the seat next to me would remain empty. The bus was packed full of students trying to get to their classes, and I was lucky enough to grab a seat by myself. My headphones were blaring in my ears, and I had my nose buried in my military history textbook. The bus stopped and I felt the presence of someone approaching my seat. It was easy trying to ignore them until they put their hand in my face as an attempt to get my attention. I looked up at them and was struck by a pair of bright green eyes. His hair was long and dark, but not as dark as Andrea's had been. He was smiling at me and it was the first time since moving here that I felt my cheeks redden at the sight of someone's smile. I saw his mouth moving, and I had to pull out my earbuds to hear him.

148

"I'm sorry?" I asked.

"I was asking if this seat was taken," he said. Even his voice took me off guard; deep and melodic. "Everywhere else is full, and I'm still nursing an old wound."

"Oh, no, go ahead. It's all yours." I struggled to talk and get out the words to answer him.

"Thanks!" I moved my bag and gave him the adjacent seat and left one headphone in just in case. My book was still open in my lap but I struggled to get back into the page. "Have you seen the most recent episode?" he asked.

"What?" I looked at him confused.

"Your bag." He pointed to the designed bag in my lap that I got because of a TV show Sam and I were watching.

"Oh, not yet, but my friend and I are going to binge the season tomorrow night." I looked up and saw the look of approval on his face.

"Well, then I won't say another word on it, but I think the two of you will enjoy it."

"I'll take your word for it," I said with a light chuckle.

The two of us talked for the entire twenty-minute bus ride to campus. We discussed books, TV shows, movies, he even asked me about my studies. I told him I wanted to be a registered nurse because of someone from my childhood. I did not tell him who, but it helped talking to someone about it. It was the first time I had brought up anything about her since elementary school, since her funeral. Miss Melody, the woman who influenced me more than my mother ever had, and the only woman I came close to feeling was like a mother to me.

The bus came to a stop and the lot of us, minus three people from the back, got off in front of the liberal arts building. I looked up at the large windows that showed the insides of the library where all of the teachers' offices were scattered amongst the labyrinth of bookshelves. It was a pain to find anything in that massive room, but it made it much easier to hide from the rest of the school. If you found a nice spot hidden amongst the shelves, no one would find you there.

"Well," he said. "Thank you for the conversation."

"You're welcome." I gave him a smile and he smiled back. I turned to walk to my class but he stopped me.

"How about we catch up later and chat some more? I'd like to get to know you a little bit."

"I have two classes this afternoon," I told him. "But I will be free after. Meet me in the student union later?"

"Sounds good to me." He let out a light chuckle. "By the way, I never caught your name," he said. I thought about it a moment and was half tempted to give him a false name, but I did not see the point in it.

"Sarah."

"That's a nice name. I'm Jacob."

"Well," I began extending a hand to him. "It's nice to meet you." He took it.

"Nice to meet you too," he beamed.

I left him standing there in front of the library doors and walked to my first afternoon class, biology. How else can someone learn about being a nurse before learning the basics? Unfortunately, it was a class I hated, and that was mainly because everything the professor taught, I already knew from high school. The only reason I had to take it was because my mother could never afford the dual credit. It gave me the entire class period to work on assignments for it and others while the instructor rambled on and on about their lecture, or for the case of biology class, their thesis. It was all I could do to not feel bored to death

150

with it.

The lecture was finally over, and I could make my way to a class that I was actually interested in, military history. It was the first day in the class with it being a half semester course, but I had been nose deep in the books for it since the beginning of the semester. The class was also a requirement for the ROTC detachment that operated through the school. I was lucky enough to snag the last seat in what they called the civilian class. It was a quick walk to the building; one that I could see from the window of my biology classroom. The two were combined by a sort of bridge that stretched over the sidewalk below, making it easy for me to avoid getting trampled by the entire student body. Most of which towered over me.

I set my book and my notebook down on the desk when I got there and buried myself in notes that I had taken in the weeks leading up to the class. It was weird not seeing more people walk in with each opening of the door. At about a minute to class time, a whole pack of others piled into the room and crowded it very quickly. My heart stopped when I saw the last person to walk through the door, Jacob. I did not know why, but he made me slightly nervous. It was hopeful to think he would find a seat somewhere in the room and avoid me altogether. What I did not anticipate was for him to set his stuff down at the teacher's desk in the front of the room. I pulled out my laptop and opened it up to the school's website to look up the class information. It kept telling me to log in, something I had not done in a long while, and was getting forced out by the same 'reset your password' phrase that hit us every couple of months.

"Good evening class," he said. "My name is Jacob Broddesson, and I'll be your instructor for the duration of this class. The university thought it would be appropriate for someone with some experience in military tactics and strategy to come teach you." He paused a moment to write down something on the board. "Now, first thing's first, where do you all think the start of military history stems from?" The class looked at him, blank expressions on their faces while he leaned fists first into the desk. "Some people say military history begins with the first form of a governed military force; my experience tells me that the first form of military history stems from the first conflict. Whether you believe that to be the conflict between Cain and Able or the first fight between early man with their wooden clubs. Military history surrounds us all. For the sake of this class, military history begins with the first shots fired in Boston Massachusetts on March 5, 1770."

*

"So," I began. "You didn't tell me that you were a teacher."

"You didn't tell me what classes you were taking," he said with a chuckle. "All that aside, I am surprised that you're taking my class considering... well, you know," he finished, gesturing to me.

"What's that supposed to mean?" I asked him.

"Well," he started. "A lot of the student demographic is either ROTC students, veterans, or military brats whose parents forced them to take it." He looked me up and down. "A lot of them are also about twice your size."

I nodded and went back to sipping on the tea he insisted he pay for. His smile had me in its grasp. I wanted to be offended by his quick judgment of me, but his smile just took me off guard and I did not know what I was mad about to begin with. It felt like a mistake to feel like this with him, and I kept thinking back to Andrea. She was the only person I had ever felt this way about before. I looked at him as he kept talking, but I was not taking in anything that he was saying, his mouth moving but being encased entirely in silence.

"I'm sorry, I've got to go!" I stood with my bag and rushed from the student union's dining hall. There was a desire to look back and see if he was watching or following me, but I was too scared to look at him.

When I hit the bus, my legs were like jelly, and I could feel my face stinging. I forgot to show the driver my travel card, and they had to come up to me and ask for it before leaving the school. 'Unknown Caller' flashed across my phone's screen, and I closed it and stuffed it into the depths of my bag. I had an idea to call Sam, but left it alone. I needed to be alone.

I rode the bus as far as the park before getting off. It was two stops from the apartment and it gave me a good excuse to walk home if I needed to and avoid being around too many people. No one ever came to the park at this time of the day leaving the fields to myself. I sat down in the grass that was still a little damp from the last sprinkler cycle. It left the field soft, and I could not resist the urge to kick off my shoes and let my feet take in the cool dirt. I laid back and let it sink through my clothes to my skin. The only thing that would have made it feel more soothing would have been one of the books on my 'to be read' list, but the ambient silence was enough for the moment. The sounds of the passing cars on the road was loud enough to hear, but also faint enough that it was not disturbing. I closed my eyes and felt like I could have been able to go to sleep and was about to when I felt the air shift around me.

"You know, when you want to be alone, you should really find a better hiding spot." I turned my head and saw Sam laying

153

right beside me.

"Let's face it," I said. "I'm doomed anyway." I turned back over and covered my face with my hands.

"What happened?" she asked

"I met a guy…" I felt her roll over on her side.

"That's what you're worried about? A guy?" The snarky tone in her voice was tangible.

"You don't get it." I felt the guilt rising again. "He's one of my class professors, and I couldn't help, but feel oddly warm and bubbly inside when I was talking to him."

"That sounds like something straight out of a porno," she said with a giggle. "And what do you mean when you say you talked to him?"

"We ran into each other on the bus, and we just started talking. Turns out, he's my military history teacher and we met up for a drink after class, and I panicked and ran out."

"I don't get it," she said. "Was there something wrong with the guy?"

"No, not at all." I let out a sigh. "He was charming."

"So, what's bothering you then? If you really like the guy and there's nothing wrong with him, why don't you see him again?" She sat up, crossed her legs, and stared down at me with her chin resting on her fists.

"It feels weird having something with someone that's not Andrea." I felt the stinging in my face again. "It feels like a betrayal."

"Sounds more like an identity crisis," Sam joked.

"You're not helping!" I said, punching her in the shoulder.

"Okay, you're right. I'm sorry," she said with a pained look. "So, you like both guys and girls then?"

"Yes… no… I don't know." I shook my head. "This is just

weird!"

"Well," she said standing up. "Let's go home, drown ourselves in ice cream and rom-coms, and see if we can figure it out."

I took her hand and she helped me to my feet. We walked side by side back to our apartment with Sam's arm over my shoulder the whole time. The streets had grown even more quiet with a car driving by us once every couple of minutes. I tilted my head back to look at the stars, but all I got was the nearly full moon shining through the streetlights above our heads. There never was a place for me to look up at the stars and I was starting to think there never would be.

*

It was another two days before I had to be in his class again. I took an earlier bus than normal and spent the time before my biology class sitting in the library in the liberal arts building. The spot I had found was a spot no one had ever bothered me in, and a spot I hoped would stay hidden from everyone. I looked out of the top floor window at the campus below. It was crazy to see so many bustling bodies hurry between buildings, strolling through without a care, or sitting on the benches by themselves or with friends.

I spotted two girls sitting together eating lunch and I thought back to all of the times I would sit with Sam. All of the talks we would have that led to all of the laughs and the jokes that her, and I would toss back and forth with one another. A third girl walked up and shared a moment with one of the first two that sent chills down my spine. She walked up, gave the first a hug then shared the same with the second before pulling her in for a kiss. They were us, all three of us. My brain was flooded with a whole new wave of memories. The first that came to mind was a night the three of us spent at Sam's when her mom had gone out of town. Sneaking the bottle of whiskey and drinking until the three of us were passed out in Sam's living room. Worst headache any of the three of us had ever had and Sam got half thrown through the house because of the missing bottle. It left much to desire if the woman who had them stashed through the house was worried about missing one.

The vibrating alarm on my phone went off to remind me about my biology class and I stood to leave. Navigating the twists and turns found me late to my classes the first couple of days followed by ridicule from both my instructors as well as the other students. My size gave them the opportunities to joke about whether or not I got on the right bus. I guess people were right; high school never ends and the only thing that changes are the people.

I spaced out during class; not working on homework or taking notes, but thinking about how I was going to sit through Jacob's class. His lecture from the last class was engaging and it helped that I was partially ogling over him. It was hard to take my eyes off of him sometimes. I was just hoping he would not want an explanation for running out on him the other day. When the time came and I sat down in his classroom, my anxiety had started to get the best of me. I sunk my face so far into my book that it would have been appropriate for me to fall into Revolutionary War America. It was not long before he walked in.

"Good afternoon, everyone. I hope you all have done the assigned reading from last class, your notes from the readings are graded and is the reason why I have you all submitting them online. Remember, history isn't just what I tell you in here, it is also what you learn through the reading and other media assigned to you."

I could not help it. My face was drawn from the pages and onto his face. His eyes were so deep of a green and his hair was a deep brown that went half to his shoulders before curling slightly on the ends. He slicked it back to keep it neat and gave a great frame for his face. He almost seemed like a short haired Andrea, and that made me feel more guilty. I back seated those thoughts of him and put my face back down into my notes, only taking in what he was saying and writing down what sounded important to me. It did not need to become known that I had already completed the semester paper and that the notes from his lectures were almost pointless. I was getting irritated with the book notes; having to go back and reread the book just to get enough information to be suitable. Finally, his lecture ended and I was able to try and flee from his classroom. At least I thought I was.

"Miss Cranston, may I speak with you a moment?" I stopped in the door as the last one in line to walk out and kept myself from looking at him. "Miss Cranston?" I stepped back and turned toward him, my eyes down at my shoes and my hands gripping the strap on my bag.

"It's Palmer." It took me a moment that my last name on my license did not match the name on the school's registrar.

"Okay, Miss Palmer. How are you?" he asked.

"Fine," I said curtly. Do not show interest, that was the plan.

"Are you sure? You had me worried there the other day when you stormed out of the union." He took a step toward me and I could not help but take a step back.

"Listen, you are a teacher of mine, and it would be

157

completely inappropriate to keep seeing you outside of class hours. It is also inappropriate of me to humor such an idea so I would like very much for you to stop as well." It came out like a flood, and I did nothing to stop it. Eventually, in the silence between us, I looked up at him and he seemed puzzled.

"I was merely seeking your friendship and I'm sorry if I caused you any trouble." He said it with a smile, it seemed genuine. "I'm also sorry if it seemed like I was coming on a little strong. I don't interact with civilians often enough and my superiors thought some time away would be appropriate."

"Superiors?" I asked. His phone went off and distracted him.

"Yeah. Sorry, I've gotta go. How about we meet up sometime later and talk about it. Coffee tomorrow morning in the union?"

"Sure," I said, not thinking about avoiding him. His mystery seemed so much more appealing to me now. "Sounds great!"

"Excellent! Here." He fished a small card from his bag and handed it to me. "My number so you know who's texting you."

"Don't you need mine?" I asked him.

"I can pull that from the roster. I'll see you tomorrow!" It started to make sense with the unknown caller from the other day. He had his back to me and was hurrying out of the classroom, leaving me there alone.

It was not the only instance. I went to the student union early to get my tea and avoid having him insist on paying again. Being independent from him helped keep my mind off of the thought of his companionship. I sat, read, sipped, and waited for him to show, but he never did. Three hours in the student union, wasted. As was the fifteen dollars I spent on tea that I had gotten tired of after the third refill. He never text me or said anything, and I spent the last half an hour serially checking my phone to see if he did.

Every ping leaving me with just another email from the university.

I ran home and cried into Sam's shoulder while she rambled on and on about how much of a jerk he was. Brad tried to be supportive, but with a girlfriend as butch as Sam, helping a crying girl was out of his wheelhouse. In the weeks following, Jacob never showed. The university assigned another teacher for his post. A teacher who changed the entire lesson plan as well as the semester paper. All of that work, down the drain, forcing me to start over on a semester's worth of work. Damn him! At least he seemed to disappear altogether, or Sam might as well have made him herself and smile in the courtroom when she pleaded innocent for it.

Lucy

The bass pounded in my ears as I sat at the bar at the frat party laughing with Sam. She just turned down ass hole number four that tried to hit on her that night. Every single one of them tried to use quirky pick-up lines, more times than not trying to win her hand in sexual favors. We were both several drinks in, but the amount of times we assaulted our livers already this semester left us with a tolerance that scared us shitless when we finally looked at the number of red cups we had gone through.

I slammed back the rest of my current glass then waved it at the bartender for another. He was cute, but not my type. Besides, he was another loser obsessed with trying to win over Sam. I turned around in my stool and made eye contact with some random guy at the other end of the room. Zoned out, I barely noticed Sam tapping me on the shoulder. I was staring at him and, weirdly enough, he was staring back. I could feel the heat rising in my cheeks and I quickly turned back around and buried my face in my hands.

"Yo! What's up with you?" Sam asked. I shook my head, failing to hide the stupid grin on my face. She poked my shoulder. "Hello? Earth to Sarah?"

"Ladies." A deep voice came from behind me and I felt a hand on my shoulder.

"Sorry, I'm not interested." Sam went straight into her turn down speech.

"Actually, I am here to make acquaintances with your

friend." I kept my face buried, but I could sense the expression on Sam's face and she was just as baffled as I was.

"Excuse us for a moment please." Sam grabbed me by the hand and pulled me away from the bar and toward the bathroom. We barged in and she locked the door behind us. "Okay, game plan. How do you want to handle this?"

"What do you mean?"

"What I mean is you are talking to him tonight!" Both of her hands were on my shoulders, and she had a dead serious expression on her face.

"Why? Give me three good reasons why I should go talk to him."

"Okay, one: he's super cute, two: he's super cute, three: he actually seems interested in you." She had a point with the last one, but why me? I was a nervous wreck when it came to relationships. I avoided Sam for over a month before actually talking to her after admitting I had a crush on her. It put a small dampener in our friendship until I met Andrea, and then there was the awkward couple of days with Jacob. "Now, you are going to go out there and let that man buy you a drink!"

"But..."

"Nope, do it!" I nodded, feeling anxious and discouraged at the same time. What was I going to say?

Sam spun me toward the door, put her hands on my shoulders, and walked me back to our spot at the bar. To my misfortune, he was still standing there. He was at least six foot, long, curly black hair, skinny but muscular. I could see the shape, his muscles made under his red button down. He saw us as we approached, a dumb grin on his face that left butterflies in my stomach.

"Welcome back."

161

"Hi…" I replied. I could feel my voice shaking with my breathing. His eyes were a deep green and absolutely gorgeous.

"Well," Sam said, "I am going to go spend some time dancing." She patted my shoulder and whispered, "good luck!" into my ear. A few more silent moments went by between us before he spoke up.

"Your friend is… something," he said.

"She's just looking out for me is all."

"Right…" he dragged. "I'm Robert, by the way." He held out a hand to me. I took it.

"Sarah." My voice was still shaking.

"Well, Miss Sarah, it is a pleasure to meet you."

"Likewise." The bartender came back with two drinks. I lifted mine and we cheered before I chugged half the glass.

"So…" I began, "are you a part of the frat?" Robert shook his head.

"Nah. I'm just the cousin that pays for it all." We both chuckled.

"If you were trying to use that line to impress me, it didn't work."

"Didn't it?" he asked, a sly smile on his face.

"You didn't need to say it." I looked over his shoulder and saw a woman that looked exactly like me. Short, blonde, a black dress that hung on a scarily thin frame, and she was barefoot. Her skin was a ghostly white.

"Are you okay?" he asked. Glancing over his shoulder to see what it was I was staring at. I nodded.

"Yeah, I am. Sorry." We both looked at each other and a compulsion came over me in a moment I could never see myself in a million years. "You wanna get out of here?" I asked. He almost looked shocked.

162

"What about your friend?"

"She does the same shit to me every other week with her boyfriend." He smirked at that.

"Very well. I know the perfect place." And away we went.

The rest of the night went by in a blur. I guess that last drink really got a hold of me. He took me back to the hotel he was staying in and brought me up to his room. The bed sheets he laid me on were soft and so was he. If I were to say we were acting on animal instinct, we were not. He held me in a loving embrace as we laid down together in that bed. I let him take me... I *wanted* him to take me, and I could feel like he wanted to take me too. It was raw, it was emotional... it was my first time with a man, and one that knew what he was doing. He was sweet, he was gentle, but Sam warned me about guys like him. I knew I was the one who called it, but he was too eager to the punch. I snuck away and back to my apartment and Sam was there in the living room to greet me when I finally got back.

"So... how was he?" she asked with a smirk. I shook my head.

"Shut up," I said, and I tossed my shoes at her.

*

I spent most of the morning camped out by the toilet puking and dry heaving whenever my body decided to. Putting me through hell against my own free will. Sam was there holding back my hair. It was the fourth day in a row I woke up like that, and I was beginning to think that it was not just the flu. Sam was in the same mindset as me, considering she was also the one who had been pointing out that I had gotten bigger over the past couple of months. I was starving myself and going to the gym

163

twice as much just to try and get back down to weight.

"Are you sure you don't want to take a test?" she asked.

"I'm sure," I said, gasping in between heaves. Then there came another one.

"No, fuck this shit," she said, and she stormed off to her room.

I sat back against the tub and pulled my knees to my chest. The heaving had finally stopped, and I was able to take in a normal breath. There was no way that I was. I did not want to believe it. *He had to have had protection, right?* The woman was there again, staring at me from the reflection in the porcelain of the toilet bowl. Her face was contorted to the curve, but her features were just as prominent. *Go away!* I shouted in my head, clenching my eyes shut to hide her face. I opened my eyes and the woman was replaced by a concerned Sam. She held a stick in hand and shoved it into my own before leaving to give me some privacy.

"You're taking one, no choice in the matter." I sighed and pulled down my shorts to take the test.

Several minutes went by before the timer on my phone went off telling me that I could look at it, and I looked at the thin pink lines on the readout. I did not want to believe it. Two pink lines were forming in the small strip at the base. I sat down on the lid of the now-closed toilet and shuddered. Sam came in and held me, looking at the test herself. I sobbed into her shoulder as we sat there for what felt like hours. She pulled away and I sniffled, wiping a sleeve across my face to wipe away the tears.

"What do you want to do?" she asked. There was only one thing I could think of doing. The woman in black was still reflecting off the backs of my eyelids.

164

*

My back was killing me, but I did not want to stay in bed all day when Sam had gotten the whole party set up for me in our apartment. Only three other people were coming, but she still wanted to have it. I called Robert the night before to see if he was coming and if he had gotten the invitation… after being sent to voicemail three times, I was sure he was not. Who needed him? I had Sam. She helped me over to the couch where all of our friends were and she began to help me with handing me some of the gifts that they brought. They were all thoughtful people and meant the world to us, but I did not really need them here. I was grateful they were.

After opening the astonishing three gifts that they brought, which consisted of bottles, diapers, and a set of blankets, they began to swarm me with questions.

"Who's the father?"

"Do you know the gender yet?"

"Are you okay with raising the baby all by yourself?"

"Have you picked out any names?"

"Guys, come on. She's only one person. Besides, Sarah has me, the best auntie in the world." She threw her arms around me in a hug.

"Oh stop," I said, lightly nudging her with my shoulder.

"Well, it is not *my* fault your family decided to keel over on ya." I winced at that. The fact that I had no blood family to turn to weighed on me more than anything. Sam must have seen the sadness in my face. My Mother I could care less for, but I wish my dad was still there to see it; to see his little girl bring life into the world. He would be the one running it while also running covert operations to 'find the scum that knocked up his little girl.'

165

"Who wants cake?" Sam asked. Everyone nodded their approval and she went away to retrieve the improvised dessert. She knew how to bake, but the effort she put into it was always a mystery. A large rectangular platter was set in front of us with red and blue frosting as well as red and blue sprinkles that coated their opposing sides.

"Sam... why is it multicolored?" I asked, looking at her.

"Oh," she began, "I forgot to tell you. I jokingly called your doctor and told her we were lesbian lovers who were having the baby together, and that I wanted to surprise you." It all came out so fast that I did not catch it all.

"What do you mean?"

"I know the gender of your baby that you refused the other day," she said, quick and sweet. I almost froze in my seat. My shoulders were shaking at the thought. The only reason I refused the information of the gender was because I was still too scared to find out what I was dealing with.

Sam handed me a knife to cut the cake with and I hesitated. In the reflection of the blade was the blonde woman I kept seeing. It made me think how much I looked like my mother. I stared at the blue and red of the toppings contemplating what I wanted to know and what I did not want to. Everyone's eyes were on me as I sat there with the knife. What did I want to know? Did I want a boy and not know how to raise him to be a man? Did I want a girl that could be raised with the same problems as me? There were too many possibilities. I let the knife slide through the cake and pulled it out to see if any crumbs were left on the blade. The only thing that came back up was the frosting and the sprinkles as they stuck to it. I finished cutting the slice and slid the knife underneath to lift it up and finally get to know the gender of my baby. I closed my eyes and, as I did so, and anticipated the reaction from my friends. A gasp echoed around the room. I slowly opened my eyes and was practically squinting at the piece of cake on the knife. What stared back at me was a dark slice of red velvet.

*

Pain. Pain was the only thing I felt surging through my body while I screamed. My legs rested in the stirrups that were pressed toward my head as the doctor kept telling me the same thing over and over again: push. Sam was there, and I was pretty sure I was breaking her hand from just how hard I was grasping it. My throat was killing me from the screaming as I continued to follow the doctor's orders. Not even a life of abuse and depression could prepare me for something like that. The more I pushed, the more pain I felt surging through me, but I kept pushing. I knew what it was and it was one of the last things I remembered. After hours of pains and what felt like even more hours of pushing, there was a large amount of relief that washed over me. Everything in my vision went white while I heard the scrambling of the doctor and the nurses. I felt weak but I did my best to listen for the small cry that I knew would have been there, but never came.

"What's… going on?" I managed to get out, but no one answered before everything faded out around me.

I finally came to, and the world around me was spinning. Bright lights shined down on me in a room I did not recognize. What happened to me? I felt around my face and my fingers came upon a plastic mask that covered my nose and mouth with tubes escaping from the front. With hands rested on the mattress, I went to sit up but was met with a soreness that wrapped through my arms and torso. I looked around the room but did not see anyone,

I recognized. Sam was gone, the doctor and the nurses were gone. I remembered being in pain. I remembered the doctor telling me to push. I remembered silence in the room once the pain finally subsided. Where was my baby? I wanted to scream for the nurses to ask them what happened, but the words were lost in my throat as the world slowly faded away again.

The second time I woke up, I was finally able to recognize my own room, and Sam was fast asleep in the chair against the wall. A book rested on her chest, *Dracula*, it was about time she got around to reading it. Finally, the fatigue was gone, and I was able to sit up in bed and properly look around the room. My mouth and my throat were dry, so I pressed the button for the nurse. I asked for a glass of water and she went away. Sam woke up in a fit, tossing her book on the floor in the process.

"Hey, you're up. How do you feel?" She stretched her arms and her shoulders popped.

"I'm fine," I whispered. I was finally able to take in the room I was in. "Where… where is she?" I looked around the room frantically, my eyes falling on the empty bassinet on the far side, and I could feel the sweat already forming on my head. My hands began to shake. Something did not feel right. "Sam… where is my baby?" Sam looked down at the floor making eye contact with the cover of the open book she had flung from her chest. "Sam!" I could feel the lump in my throat as she stood and walked over to me, wrapping me in a tight hug.

"I am so, so sorry, Sarah…" She sobbed into my shoulder, and I could not stop myself from breaking down too. It was finally coming to me. The silence in the room after the relief. The anxiousness and hurriedness of the doctor and the nurses. Why did the world always take everything away from me?

Over Sam's shoulder stood the blonde woman, frowning,

168

and holding an infant in her arms.

*

A cold autumn wind chilled my fingertips and nipped at my nose and my cheeks. Red and orange leaves littered the ground around my feet and formed blankets over the stones in the field, hiding the names of their owners, but I knew where I was going. Straight back thirteen rows from the gate then down twenty-three stones from the path on my left. The wind whipped my hair around my head causing streaks of auburn hair to whip past my eyes, making it difficult to focus. I adjusted the bouquet of roses in my arm to let me pull out a scrunchie from my pocket and tie the long strands back into a loose tail. I continued counting; twenty-one, twenty-two, twenty-three. I looked down at the stone tablet laying at my feet and felt my breathing grow ragged. The tears tickled my cheeks as I wept silently. Kneeling down, I went to brush away the leaves but stopped myself. I glanced at the next stones on my left. I knew whose they were, and I did not want to leave anything for them, well, one of them. The other I cursed myself for not bringing another bundle of flowers though he never really cared for them. I moved the leaves away from his stone with my hand revealing the etchings:

George Palmer
July 22, 1973 – March 6, 2022

"Hi, dad," I whispered.
"You know he was a liar and a cheat right, Sarah?"
"So, you finally speak to me after all this time." I kept my gaze down and away from the familiar voice.

"What, no warm, welcoming greetings for your dear old mother?"

"The fuck do you want?" I looked up at her, the woman who had been haunting me since that night in the bar. Her blonde hair had thinned as did her body. She looked sick with her cheeks sunken in to reveal the bones. Her feet were still bare as she made her way toward me from her own stone. She stopped and looked up past my eyes and above my forehead.

"What have you done to your hair?"

"I dyed it. I needed to remove the remnants of you. At least with auburn hair, I know it won't be myself that I'm looking at in the mirror when I see you." She nodded and looked down at Dad's grave.

"If I could still spit..."

"Fuck off." I moved past her and placed a single rose in the steel vase.

"Do you really hate me that much?" she asked with her head cocked to one side.

"You certainly didn't do anything for me not to..."

"I busted my ass to provide for you!" she screamed, interrupting me again. She was always interrupting me.

"You brought in a trust-fund pedophile and watched blindly as he took advantage of me while you sat there doped up and drunk off your ass!" Silence fell between us as the wind blew past our ears. I could feel the heat rising in my face.

"How dare you? I am your mother," she finally said.

"You're a parasite." I knelt down in front of the grave that I was there to see. It would have been her birthday.

"What did you name her?" she asked.

"You should know," I snapped. "You were the first one who got to hold her despite being in hell."

"Yeah I do," she said angrily. "I want to hear you say it." I looked back over at the stone and shook my head.

"I can't." There was no way that I could say it.

"Huh… pity." Her condescending tone was irritating. Typical of her.

"What do you know? All you have ever done for me is belittle me, allow people to abuse me, and why? All so you could get your fix!" I took a breath. "You never cared, and I don't want you to. I don't *need* you to." I stood up and began walking away from the woman I never knew. "You were never there before. Why do I need you here now?"

"I guess that's the real question isn't it?" I glanced over my shoulder and she was gone. Good riddance.

I knelt at the foot of the stone and wiped away the leaves.

"Hey! You good, Sarah?" I looked back and saw Sam coming my way.

"Yeah. I'm good." I wiped the tears from my eyes.

"Who were you talking to?" I looked at my mother's stone.

"Nobody."

"Right… anyway, are you ready? Don't forget, we still have your going away party tonight."

"Do we have to?" I groaned.

"Yes, because I could only get all of us together for one last hoorah."

"Fine." I looked back down at the stone and set the roses at the head of the inscription.

Lucy Palmer
November 19, 2026 – November 20, 2026